Freezing Heart

"Rachel!" he exclaimed. "Darling – how wonderful. This is the best, easily the best Christmas present you could possibly have given me. But – but how did you manage it? Oh, I can't believe it's really you!"

And then he was pulling her into his arms and kissing her – a long, passionate kiss, a mixture of tenderness and deep, deep longing. For a few moments, Rachel allowed herself to sink into the warmth, the wonderful sensation of being with Jack again, of being loved by him.

Then she remembered all that had happened, and anger took over once again. "Look – I think I deserve an explanation," she said. "Jack – are you completely crazy, or is it me?"

Freezing Heart

Amber Vane

■ SCHOLASTIC

Scholastic Children's Books
Commonwealth House, 1–19 New Oxford Street,
London WC1A 1NU, UK
a division of Scholastic Ltd
London ~ New York ~ Toronto ~ Sydney ~ Auckland

First published by Scholastic Ltd, 1996

Copyright © Amber Vane, 1996

ISBN 0 590 13600 3

Typeset by TW Typesetting, Midsomer Norton, Avon

Printed by Cox & Wyman Ltd, Reading, Berks.

1

It was just like flying, Rachel thought excitedly, as she skimmed through the glistening snow, her cheeks glowing, her whole being lit up and glad to be alive. If you looked up you might have thought it was midsummer, the sky was such a startling blue, the sun so dazzling. And yet all around were these white slopes, the spectacular snow-covered mountains, the little wooden houses perched on the hills. And the strange glow in the air was the reflection of the sun on snow drifts and icy peaks.

Rachel was so pleased with her progress down the nursery slope that she decided to try something a little more ambitious – she directed her skis sharply to the left, then to the right, until she was zooming downwards in a mad zigzag, faster and faster until she was completely out of control. That was when she panicked, lost her rhythm, jerked the wrong way, and toppled right over, landing in an undignified heap in a thick bank of snow, her skis flailing helplessly in the air.

A peal of giggles broke out behind her. She managed to squirm round enough to see her best friend Lisa perched on her sticks, shaking with laughter. Eventually Lisa staggered over to offer Rachel a helping hand. "Ooh, you look just like a spider!" she hooted as she hauled her friend upright. "Except spiders don't usually have pink and green stripes all over their backs."

Rachel, who was rather proud of her new snazzy snow suit, scowled at Lisa. "Oh, I expect the really deadly ones do," she answered. "And they always go for creatures of vulgar colours. Like bright orange for instance."

Lisa was, of course, dressed from top to toe in a flame-coloured all-in-one suit. A matching hat perched on her blonde curls. She grinned good-temperedly. "Just let them try," she retorted. "They'll find that spiders aren't the only females to bite off the heads of their mates."

Rachel was trying to shake the snow off her trousers, hampered by the heavy skis on her feet. She looked so funny that Lisa started laughing all over again. "Come on, softie!" she called. "Don't you know that the first rule of skiing is that when you've taken a tumble you have to get right on in there and have another go?"

The girls clambered up the slope sideways, as they'd been taught, this time making their way to the very top. "Aren't we lucky?" panted Rachel as they went. "Together yet again – and in the most fabulous place ever."

She and Lisa had been working as holiday representatives for the same company, Dream

Ticket, for nearly two years, and they always managed to end up in the same resort, though they'd never worked on a skiing holiday before.

"They must think we work well together," commented Lisa. "Or maybe Sergeant Major's got a soft spot for us after all."

She was referring to Janice Ingham, the long-suffering manager at Dream Ticket's headquarters in London. She was responsible for allocating all the reps to the different package holidays, and although she'd been doing it for years, ruling the whole chaotic operation with great dedication, she always seemed to be flustered and in crisis. Rachel and Lisa had got used to her perpetual panics and her conviction that something, somehow, was going to go terribly wrong.

"Now I'm not at all sure I'm doing the right thing, sending you off to Edelweiss," she'd fussed. "I mean, neither of you has worked on a ski tour before and you won't find it easy. Not at all easy." She drew in her breath sharply as if predicting a terrible hurricane or a famine. Then she sighed. "But I suppose I don't have any choice. Bookings have been left to the last minute as per usual. Why the public can't plan its holidays in a nice, organized fashion, six months ahead of time as recommended in our brochure, I'll never know. So I suppose we'll just have to make the best of it. You two had better book into our winter holiday training module where you will be given basic instruction in skiing and snow-boarding, elementary German, winter first aid and of course cookery and hostessing skills."

"What skills?" squawked Rachel in alarm.

"Oh, yes," Janice said severely. "I told you it was no picnic. These are our middle to up-scale range of holiday chalets for fun-lovers with that little extra to spend." Whenever Janice started talking like the company's brochures, Rachel and Lisa would get the giggles. Now, they were desperately trying to keep their faces straight as she carried on her sales pitch.

"We like to think of our reps as hosts as well as guides," Janice explained. "That means that you'll be in charge of the smooth running of the chalets and you'll supervise the chalet staff who do the cooking and light housework. You will, naturally, need to know the basics and from time to time you may be expected to join in with those little extras – special cakes for tea, gourmet puddings, tasteful arrangement of the luxury cheeseboard, that kind of thing. Our ideal is for our guests to look on you as part of the family..."

As they edged towards the top of the slope, Rachel reminded Lisa of Janice's words. "Remember we're supposed to be hosts, guides and – what was that last one?"

"Part of the family," supplied Lisa. "I hope that doesn't mean we end up looking like them. Especially the Pink lot!"

There were six chalets in Edelweiss, a little settlement in the midst of a whole network of ski runs and slopes, dotted with villages and resorts. Dream Ticket had named them after colours, and Lisa had already taken against the Pink chalet for some reason.

"I don't know how you can make up your mind so quickly," Rachel laughed. "They only got off the plane this morning."

"That's all I needed," Lisa said darkly. "Ten of them, all in a group, all booked in together – and all of them nearly old enough to be my parents. I mean, two of them were actually holding hands like some romantic couple. It's disgusting. I think they should ban sex once you reach 30. After that, it should just be chocolate and a little light gardening."

"Just wait till you get there," Rachel warned her, laughing. "Anyhow, thank goodness they won't be our responsibility. Marjorie's doing Pink and Blue." Marjorie was the local resort manager, in charge of all the reps and chalet staff. She managed two of the chalets, leaving four for Rachel and Lisa with two other reps, Jason and Gudrun. All of them had met the Dream Ticket charter plane at Salzburg that morning and had settled their charges, allocating rooms and explaining all the details of the holiday. Now, they were enjoying a very brief break before they'd have to meet everyone in the bar for the official welcome.

There was a sudden rush of sound as a startling vision in black and purple whizzed past them. "Hi, Gudrun!" shouted Lisa, waving after the apparition who was now disappearing down the slope, her long blonde hair flying behind her. It was hard to tell whether she had acknowledged the greeting.

"Not all that friendly, is she?" sniffed Rachel.

"Oh, give her a chance," reasoned Lisa. "It's great to have a real German-speaker on board. And besides, I always like meeting people from other countries. It's part of the fun."

"Yes, well, that depends who," said Rachel. "She doesn't exactly come over as a bundle of fun, you have to admit."

"Great skier, though," Lisa said admiringly, watching Gudrun's effortless curves and sweeps in the snow. "I wish I could do that. I've only just managed those parallel turns and just look at her! She makes it look so easy. I'm going to have a go."

"Lisa, don't go too crazy," Rachel warned her anxiously. "I don't want to have to send out rescue dogs with brandy round their neck to sniff you out from under some avalanche. Not on the first day…"

But Lisa wasn't listening. She stood poised for a moment at the top of the slope, legs bent, sticks in the air. And then she was off, careering down the mountainside in a series of wild sweeps.

"This is great!" she cried to Rachel.

"Watch out!" Rachel yelled back, watching her friend gathering more and more speed and weaving precariously in and out of other skiers dotted along the way. But her warning was too late. Lisa, racing faster and faster down the slope, had finally lost all control and had crashed unceremoniously into the arms of the hapless skier who happened to be crossing her wayward path.

"Hey!" he shouted in surprise as she thudded against him. For a second or two they rocked from side to side, desperately trying to keep their balance. And then they tumbled into the snow in a heap of arms, skis and sticks.

"Sorry," gasped Lisa after a moment. She found herself staring into a pair of irresistibly twinkling blue eyes set in a suntanned, smiling face, unmistakably handsome even though its owner was wearing one of the silliest woollen hats Lisa had ever seen. It even had a red bobble on the top!

"That is OK," he replied with a grin. "I can see you are going to be very good for business."

"Business?" Lisa echoed.

"Of course," he shrugged. "I am ski instructor for the Edelweiss ski school."

"Oh, but that's great!" Lisa exclaimed. Then she corrected herself. "I mean, that's a coincidence. I'm a rep for Dream Ticket, and all our clients use your ski school. We'll be signing them in first thing tomorrow."

"And how about you?" Bobble-hat enquired, still grinning. "You I think I could teach a great deal?"

Lisa blushed. "Well we don't strictly get the time to attend the school," she explained. "But we do get the afternoons to ourselves..."

"Good. Then tomorrow, I teach you," he said firmly. He stood up and reached out a padded, gloved hand to pull Lisa to her feet. When she was upright, he didn't let go, but solemnly shook the wrist he was gripping. "My name is Jean-Pierre Victoire," he introduced himself. "I am from Switzerland, and I promise you I am the best ski instructor in these mountains."

He pointed across the slope to where Gudrun was performing what looked like a complicated arabesque in the snow. "You see that girl? She is a good skier, very graceful. You – I can make you as good as that, no?"

Lisa nodded vigorously. Then she remembered Rachel. "Oh, but I'll be with my friend," she said loyally. "Can you do it in twos?"

Jean-Pierre grinned even more broadly. "Better and better," he said. "Two beautiful English girls – one lucky Swiss boy. I teach you to ski, you teach me – er, something very British. To dance, maybe? To drink beer? We'll think of something. Until then – *à bientôt!*"

"Er, yeah – *à bientôt!* See you tomorrow, then," Lisa said, as she made her way back to where Rachel stood waiting for her.

"Yess!" she chortled to Rachel when she caught up with her. "By the way, what does '*à bientôt*' mean?"

Rachel laughed. "Don't worry, it's nothing too compromising. It just means 'see you later'."

Lisa grinned. "This is definitely going to be the start of something good..."

2

"Good afternoon, everyone, and welcome to your first tea in Red Chalet. This is a time of day when we can all get together to swap stories and talk about our adventures. And I know you'll find that after a strenuous day on the piste there's nothing more wonderful than a real English cuppa and lots of hot buttered scones."

Rachel was beaming brightly as she addressed her guests, but it was hard to keep up the cheery tone. There were too many glares, for a start. And at least two of her group seemed to be in tears. It was more like the setting for a horror story, she thought gloomily, than the first day of a carefree skiing holiday in the Austrian Alps.

"Well I think it's rather vulgar to serve English tea," interrupted a tall, angular woman with jet black hair and very scarlet lipstick. Extraordinary turquoise globes fringed with gold dangled from her ears, wobbling dramatically as she flung back her head in disdain. Rachel, always very quick to know her clients, had already jotted down some cryptic lines about this one in her notebook. *Jonquil Redbone, jewellery designer. Could be a bit of a snob? Doesn't think she belongs on a package holiday.*

Even as she spoke, Jonquil was selecting tiny chocolate éclairs with her long, immaculately polished red nails, and biting into them with delicate greed. Her companion, boyish, good-looking, and rather younger than she was, grinned good-humouredly as he munched his way through a plate of sandwiches.

A tall, rather overbearing man in his thirties cleared his throat as if he was used to being listened to. Rachel recognized him as Brett Redbone, Jonquil's brother.

"Look, I don't really think we need all this matey get-together nonsense," he said briskly. "Just tell us how to get to the slopes and we'll just get on with it, shall we? Oh, and you might as well give us an idea about what there is to do in the evenings in this God-forsaken little hole."

Rachel held her breath and counted to ten, just as she had trained herself to do whenever troublesome clients became impossible, and carried on with her introduction as though there had been no interruptions.

"I do very much hope that you'll treat the chalet as your home while you're here with us in Edelweiss. And as you have chosen the shared accommodation option I trust you'll regard every-one in the chalet as one big family. Now, Heidi over there – " she gestured to a young Austrian woman hovering in the corner, her cheeks flushed with shyness – "Heidi will be coming in every day to clean the rooms and prepare your three meals – breakfast, tea and supper. You'll take lunch on the slopes where you'll find plenty of restaurants with something for every palate."

"Hmm – that would be a surprise," muttered Brett. The young woman at his side tossed her long, blonde hair so that it shimmered, and squeezed his arm warningly. But he just threw it off impatiently and ignored her. Rachel noted the look of hurt on her face and remembered that she was a late addition to the Redbone booking. She'd better find out why.

There was a sudden crash, followed by a shriek. A young woman in a big sweatshirt emblazoned with silver hearts had dropped her cup of tea on to the polished floor. Crouching over to pick up the pieces of broken china, she'd cut her finger and was sucking the wound distractedly as Heidi rushed over to mop up the mess.

As Janet Maple stood forlornly nursing her finger, her husband Sean looked on disinterestedly from a few feet away. "Honestly, Janet," he said languidly. "Trust you!"

"My finger really throbs," she whined. "You could be a bit more sympathetic."

"Yes, that's not very nice, Sean," put in another girl, Laura, who clearly knew them both very well. "Poor Janet's hurt herself. Again. Come on, Jan, let's go and find you a plaster." As they left the room and made their way upstairs, Rachel overheard her whispering: "Janet, you've got to

pull yourself together. We're here to enjoy ourselves, remember! Sean doesn't want to have to
worry about you the whole time. Men don't like
that..."

"I can't believe I've landed such a bunch of
misfits," Rachel confided, half an hour later, to
her boyfriend Jack Woodford. She was curled up
on the bed, cradling the phone against her
shoulder, wishing he could be there with her.

"I wish I could be there with you," he said
caressingly, just as if he could read her mind. "I
miss you so much, Rachel. I can't enjoy anything
without you any more. I miss your kisses. I miss
the way you lick your lips when you drink wine. I
miss your gorgeous legs and the way you walk too
fast so I have to run to keep up with you. I even
miss your sweet, tactless way of telling people
they're wrong and you're right."

"Ooh, that's not fair," Rachel protested, giggling.
"It's you who does that!"

He laughed softly. "OK, we both do. It's just
another thing we have in common, which is why
we get on so well. But look – here's something you
do that I don't do. You complain about the clients,
right?"

"Well you should see them!" Rachel retorted.
"I've got Jonquil the snobby jewellery designer,
plus her toy boy. Then there's her overbearing
brother the banker, and his girlfriend who looks
as if she's been crying all the time. Oh, and did I
mention the one who is actually crying all the
time – Janet, the unhappy wife whose husband

ignores her, plus their two friends Laura and Mike who look as if they're really his friends. Oh, and one normal couple called Andrea and Keith who soon won't be normal because they're surrounded by lunatics."

"Don't take it all so seriously," soothed Jack. "They're clients, that's all. You just have to be sweet to them for two weeks and they'll be gone. You know you can do that. I'm sure you'll have them tamed in no time."

Rachel felt warm inside just hearing his voice. As long as she and Jack were together nothing else really mattered – even if he was sixty miles away.

They'd met the previous summer when she and Lisa had been working in Spain. Jack had been their manager and at first she'd hated him, resenting his arrogant, bossy attitude. But then they had somehow, magically, fallen in love. She smiled now, remembering how all that hostility and dislike had transformed into passion.

"We will stay together, like this – no matter what happens. Won't we?" Jack had whispered the last time he'd held her in his arms. They'd been saying goodbye for the winter because Jack had been posted to Grossburg, the central resort for all Dream Ticket's Austrian ski holidays. He was manager for the whole district – a big promotion, but it meant that he'd be really busy right up to March, when the snow would melt.

Now, hearing his voice murmuring down the telephone, Rachel wished desperately that she could be with him, touch him, bury herself in his arms.

"You will be able to visit soon, won't you?" she pleaded, suddenly tearful.

"I'll do my best," he promised. "You know I want to be with you for Christmas. But I can't promise. There's so much to do here. Gotta go now. Bye darling. Love you."

It was five o'clock, the precious gap between tea and dinner duties, and the four reps were sitting together in the deserted Alpine Bar in the Northern Heights leisure complex. This was really a central meeting place for all the Dream Ticket clients. Sixty of them were staying in chalets, and another 100 or so in a couple of nearby hotels. All round the valley were other little holiday settlements, and there were others right across this area of the mountains, all linked by a network of ski runs and cable cars.

Northern Heights consisted of a set of low-beamed, wooden buildings housing a swimming pool and sauna, a bar and café, a medical centre, indoor sports room and gym, and an enquiry office where you could leave messages or get information about local tourist attractions. The reps were supposed to take it in turns to man the office each afternoon.

"But I can't possibly see how we're going to manage that," complained Lisa. "Not on top of everything else."

"I know – it's typical, isn't it?" agreed Rachel. "We all set out thinking we know exactly what the job is, and the minute we get here it all changes."

"Ah, you English – always complaining. I don't

see a problem. It is all very easy." This was Gudrun, the blonde, very attractive German girl who Rachel had already decided was far too cool and standoffish.

"The problem is, we were told that our job was to supervise the chalet staff. Now we find we are the chalet staff," pointed out Rachel. "And that's on top of doing all rep jobs, getting everyone to the slopes, booking their lessons, fastening their boots, sorting out their insurance when they break their legs…"

When they'd arrived, the day before, Marjorie, the local manager, had explained very apologetically that things had changed just a little. "You know what it's like," she'd said vaguely. "Probably there was a sudden rush on chalet girls and there weren't enough trained cooks to send out here."

"Or maybe Dream Ticket was suddenly too mean to cough up the money," Lisa had whispered to Rachel.

"Anyway!" Marjorie had beamed. "We've organized some local people to do the housework and prepare the food, but we'd like you to act as special Dream Ticket hosts this season. Which means doing some cooking yourselves as well as supervising your helper, and generally making everyone feel at home. Yes, it will be on top of your other duties which makes it marvellous training for you lucky young people, doesn't it?"

"Actually, I'm quite pleased," Jason confessed now, as they sat in the bar sipping steaming glasses of hot chocolate, topped with mountains of whipped cream. He was about the same age as

Rachel and Lisa – just 19 – but looked younger, probably because he wasn't very tall and had a round, innocent face with enormous eyes and a sweet smile.

They all looked at him, startled. "Yes, well, don't laugh," he said in his soft, Northern voice. "I love cooking, always have. I want to go to college and learn to be a chef. But I'm repping for a couple of years just to get some money together. This'll be great for me."

"And me," put in Gudrun unexpectedly. "Cooking is a good skill. In Germany we learn it in school, girls and boys. But also I did a Cordon Bleu course last summer so I am glad to get some practice."

Rachel and Lisa looked at each other helplessly. "Erm – I can do a mean spaghetti," volunteered Rachel. "And chips. And I'm OK with anything that doesn't require whipping or rolling."

"Oh, well, you'll be no good to me, then," quipped Jason. Rachel and Lisa laughed. Gudrun stared at him blankly, and Rachel wondered whether she disapproved of his joke, or simply hadn't quite understood it. Suddenly, she felt sorry for Gudrun. It must be hard to make friends with a group of people from another country, having to struggle by in their language. It was unfair to judge her so quickly.

"You are lucky, Gudrun," she said warmly. "You seem to be good at so many things. Languages, cooking – and I saw you out on the slopes this afternoon, you were just fantastic. You made me feel like such a klutz. I can get down the slopes all right, but I always feel as if I'm about to wobble."

Gudrun nodded, acknowledging the compliment. "I like to do things properly," she said shortly. Rachel wanted to slap her in the face for being so smug, but she told herself that was unreasonable. Lisa was right. She deserved a chance.

Lisa had turned to Gudrun and Jason and was saying eagerly: "Well, I'm not really that much of a cook either. They did teach us the basics on the training module but it wasn't a lot of use to me because I'm a vegetarian, you see."

"And she's a total born-again health freak," Rachel added affectionately. "It's amazing she's even drinking that hot chocolate without checking that it was made from organic beans! Show Lisa a gourmet dinner for two and she'll have her calculator out, adding up the E-numbers. She's so worried about insecticides she thinks they have them on strawberry ice-creams."

"You exaggerate I think," remarked Gudrun, who obviously took everything very literally. "It is good to be healthy, no?" She turned to Lisa. "I know a very good way to make vegetable lasagne. I will show you, yes?"

"Yes, but when?" groaned Lisa. "How are any of us going to find time for anything with all these extra duties?"

"Tell you what," suggested Rachel, the organizer. "We'll each take charge of one chalet, as Marjorie told us. But maybe we can share some of the duties. You know – get the chalet staff to prepare mountains of vegetables for us all to muck in with a giant stew. That kind of thing."

"Well, I'm not certain it would be entirely

satisfactory for my special hollandaise sauce," protested Jason. "I was rather hoping to try a few experiments."

"We will manage," Gudrun assured him. Rachel had the impression that she'd be saying that even if they were the last survivors in a plane crash and all their supplies had disappeared in a freak avalanche. Gudrun turned to her with an appraising look.

"So, Rachel, if you do not like the cooking and you are not so confident on the ski slopes what is your special skill?" she asked. "What do you like about the job?"

Rachel felt suddenly glad they weren't those plane crash survivors. Somehow, she was sure she would have ended up being the one they had to eat to stay alive.

"Oh, the people, really," she answered vaguely. "I really enjoy meeting all kinds of different people and helping them sort out their problems." Then, remembering her first encounter that afternoon with the strange assortment of holiday-makers who had been allotted to her chalet, she added: "Course, some crowds can be more difficult than others. My lot look as if they're going to be a bit of a handful."

At that moment a tall, rather arrogant-looking man strode into the bar and made his way to their table. Without even greeting her, Brett Redbone towered above Rachel, brows knitted, and began berating her. "What kind of a bloody useless set-up is this?" he began in a loud, sneering voice. "There's no hot water, I can't get the shower to work, and there don't seem to be any towels. And that's just since we arrived this morning. God knows what else is in store for us in this cheap little hole. I said we should have gone somewhere classier and I was right. Clearly!"

Rachel clapped her fist dramatically to her forehead in mock grief and contrition. "Oh, how stupid of me. How could I have abandoned you like this in your moment of need? Obviously I should have explained to you far more carefully how things work over here, abroad. You'll notice, you see, that there's a blue part of the dial and a red part. The blue gives you cold water and as you move towards the red the water gets hotter. It's awfully complicated but by the end of the fortnight you'll probably get the hang of it. Now the shower – well, yes, I can see why you had difficulty there and it's entirely my fault. There's a little metal plug, you see, very easy to miss as it's right next to the tap. Now, listen carefully or you may get mixed up. If you push it in you get a bath, if you pull it out you get a shower. I know, foreigners do make life difficult, don't they?"

A hush had descended as Rachel launched into her monologue. Now, pausing for breath, she was aware that everyone was staring at her. The man standing angrily before her was speechless with rage. Something told her she probably shouldn't say any more, but when Rachel was in a temper it was impossible to stop the flow. So she swept on: "And what was the other disaster? Oh, yes – towels. Again, complete oversight on my part and on behalf of the company and myself I really must apologize profusely for being so very misleading. The towels are in a ridiculously obscure place. In the airing cupboard next to the bathroom. Silly, isn't it?"

Without a word, the furious man turned heel and stalked away. There was an awed pause. Then Gudrun commented acidly: "So this is the famous English courtesy. I can see, Rachel, I have much to learn from you about the finer points of charm."

"Well, he was very rude to her," Jason put in loyally. "I think you did brilliantly, Rachel. A bit over the top maybe – but good for you."

"And look on the bright side," added Lisa. "You were complaining before that your chalet was full of horrible women. Now you don't have to worry about the sex imbalance any more."

3

"OK everyone?" Rachel called across the throng of eager faces. "Then let's get going!" As she and Lisa led the way up the snowy path to the slopes, with twenty thermal-coated holiday-makers trudging after her, she muttered darkly: "I never thought I'd have so much respect for nursery school teachers. Imagine having to do this every day!"

"Oh, it's definitely worse for us," Lisa replied. "At least they're allowed to tell the little horrors off sometimes. We have to fit their boots, fit their skis, soothe their tantrums and calm their fears – while smiling and not losing our tempers. What a job! Give me summer sun contracts any day."

At that moment the handsome skier they'd met yesterday whooshed past them, giving a friendly wave as he went and calling: "Don't forget. I give you special training this afternoon!"

Lisa blushed. "Oh, well – every job has its compensations, I suppose..."

"Lisa!" Rachel gasped. "You're not really going to meet him are you? What about Alex?"

Lisa looked defiant. "Oh, for heaven's sake, Rachel. I'm only going to go skiing with him. It hardly counts as a passionate affair. So I don't see what it has to do with Alex."

"It's because of the look on your face," Rachel said knowingly. "I get the feeling that any minute now you're going to be checking up on his vitamin intake and fretting about his biorhythms."

They both laughed. Alex had been a rep with them in Spain that summer – the summer when Jack had been their boss. He and Lisa had had a few misunderstandings before they finally got together but Rachel always claimed that Lisa should have known all along what she felt about Alex because she was so concerned about his love of junk food. "Accept it," she told her. "Some women get a shiver down their spine. Others go weak at the knees. Some lose their appetite. But for you, when you're serious about a guy, you get all motherly and want to control their diet."

Now, as they made their way carefully up the first slope, Rachel gave her friend a searching look. "Have you spoken to Alex lately, by the way?"

Lisa grinned. "This morning, actually. It was a terrible line but he sounded OK. Poor Alex, stuck in the Canary Islands on some beach, surrounded by palm trees. He actually tried to claim he was working hard. Him! What a cheek, when you look at what we're going through!"

At that moment both girls were distracted. Lisa's lively bunch of ten single young people demanded her attention because they'd made up a marching song and wanted her to join in. And Rachel, meanwhile, felt a tug on her sleeve. She turned round to see Janet Maple's plaintive face.

"Rachel, I'm sorry to be a bother, but I'm sure these boots are too small."

Rachel sighed and composed her face to look patient and understanding. "I don't think they are, Janet. Remember how long we took to fit them? Remember how careful we were and how many times you walked up and down to be absolutely sure?"

"Well they were comfortable then, but now they're pinching my feet. Can we go back?"

"Let's see if you can live with them just for today," Rachel suggested gently. "I'm sure they'll be just fine."

"If I must," Janet sniffed, clearly seeing herself as a noble martyr. "I don't want to be any trouble, obviously. But it's funny, I could swear the ones we picked had red stitching round the sides, and these have yellow. Are you sure you picked up the right ones?"

For a moment Rachel felt worried. Had she got the boots mixed up? But it was too late to go back now, so she just reassured Janet and carried on leading the group to the slopes. She noticed Gudrun striding ahead, confidently leading her ten very athletic-looking chalet members. *How had she managed to get them ready so swiftly?* Rachel wondered, remembering how she'd eyed Gudrun enviously as they'd worked side by side earlier that morning.

By now, everyone was mingling with other groups making their way up the hills. With a practised eye she picked out her own ten charges. Janet was trying to catch up with Sean and his friends, limping pathetically as she called after them. Brett and his young girlfriend Nina seemed to be getting on very well after the tensions of the first day. They were holding hands as they went, their skis locking together on their shoulders from time to time, forcing them even closer together.

"Honestly, he must be going through his mid-life crisis ten years early," Jonquil remarked loudly to Tommy. "What does he think he's doing with that – that brat?"

"Oh, I think he knows what he's doing all right," smirked Tommy. "I don't know what's worrying you Jonky – are you afraid he's going to spend all his money on her?"

"Don't be vulgar!" Jonquil snapped. "Of course not. Though naturally one worries how long he's going to be able to keep her in chewing gum and acne cream."

"Oh, miaow!" drawled Tommy good-naturedly. "Just because she's a few years younger you've got it in for her. But give the kid a chance, Jonky. She's kind of sweet. And we might as well try and enjoy ourselves while we're here…"

As they reached the slopes there was another rush of activity as people were allotted their instructors and told where to board the ski lifts to their various lessons. There seemed to be hundreds of luminous ski suits milling around, swarming in all directions. Rachel was so busy trying to organize her own group that she lost her footing and fell into a deep pile of snow.

A strong arm gripped hers and hauled her to her feet. She found herself looking into the eyes of a very bronzed, rugged face. Her rescuer had golden hair and piercing blue eyes which twinkled at her as he steadied her in the snow.

"Aha! A piece of good fortune tumbling into my path!" he exclaimed, his perfect English enhanced by a lilting Nordic accent.

Rachel grinned. "I seem to have fallen on my feet, thanks to you."

"My pleasure." The blue eyes bored into hers for a moment before the handsome face relaxed into a broad smile. "Now, don't tell me – you're from Dream Ticket, yes? Am I right – or what?"

"How did you know?" demanded Rachel, laughing.

"Easy," her rescuer shrugged. "They always have the most beautiful reps. I do not know how they manage it, but I am very glad they do. Now, I have work." Rachel noticed that he had a large, professional-looking camera slung over his shoulder. He gestured over to the thronging parties of skiers. "Maybe some would like their pictures taken, no? Everyone here, they like to take home a photo that makes them look like they are in the Olympics. But my best pictures, they are always when someone takes a somersault into the snow. This makes for very good composition."

Rachel laughed again, as he strode off up the slope. Over his shoulder, he called back to her: "I see you again, no? Come down to Karl's Place and

I give you the best hot chocolate you ever tasted. Bye for now, my English friend."

"Don't even think about it," hissed a voice behind her. Rachel turned to face a cheerful-looking English girl with a mop of bright red hair and wide green eyes. "That is the biggest flirt you'll ever meet, Karl Husser the Danish pastry."

"How do you know?" Rachel asked, curious.

"Oh, this is my third year at Edelweiss so believe me, I know. I'm Tammy Thorn by the way."

"Rachel Stanford," Rachel introduced herself.

"Well, Rachel, take my advice and keep away from the marauding Viking. I work for Conquest Holidays and all our reps call him the Town Louse."

"Why did you call him a Danish pastry?" Rachel wanted to know.

"Number one, because he's Danish. Number two, because he owns a little pâtisserie – a very little pâtisserie, but the only one with a bar attached. And as you've noticed, he fancies himself as a photographer as well. Or you might just say he fancies himself."

"What are the pastries like?" Rachel asked.

"Supremely delicious. And, before you ask, his hot chocolate is sensational. But like I said, don't get too close. The man's a menace. Plus he's a Virgo and you know what they can be like let loose on a mountain full of women. So, how are you finding Dream Ticket?"

"Well, I love repping, but this is my first winter snow run and frankly I'm finding it quite hard going," Rachel confided.

"Don't worry, everyone does at first," sympath-ized Tammy. "Especially if you're working the chalets. I'm doing hotels, which is much easier. Still, Dream Ticket always seems to be fun, and you get much dishier guys than we do. Talking of which, who is that?"

She was staring at Jason, who was making his way towards Rachel, looking bewildered. "I've lost all of mine," he said looking sorry for himself. "One minute there they all were, boots, skis, everything. Following me in a nice neat crocodile. Now they've vanished and how am I ever going to know if they've ended up in the right lessons?"

"Don't worry," chimed in Tammy. "They're not children – they'll sort themselves out. I'm Tammy Thorn, by the way. I work for your deadly rivals, Conquest. But, look, come with me and I'll show you a quick way to work out how they grade the skiers. That way, you'll easily discover where they all are."

Rachel had to admire Tammy's quick moves as she watched them disappear into the crowds. Miraculously, the muddle seemed to be turning into some kind of order, as the various ski instruc-tors began to marshal their classes and lead them to different parts of the slopes, or to the ski lifts. Jean-Pierre, she noticed, seemed to have landed the whole of Gudrun's group.

Lisa suddenly appeared by her side. "I've been checking it all out," she announced proudly. "Gudrun's got a whole set of German athletes, lucky thing. They all booked together, they belong to some kind of sports club and they're dead keen.

27

That's why they're with Jean-Pierre. He's the most experienced instructor here."

"Well, it's always wise to choose the best," Rachel said sarcastically. "I suppose he's planning to teach you a few advanced techniques during your private sessions?"

Lisa blushed, then grinned mischievously. "Let's hope so. A little brushing up is exactly what I need."

It was a glorious afternoon – the snow on the mountains glistening in the dazzling sun, the sky a deep, cloudless blue. Lisa had never felt so exhilarated. There was something about the warmth of the sun and the sharpness of the snow that filled her with energy. And then, of course, there was the added excitement of this lithe, gorgeous guy skimming along beside her, urging her to perform more and more daring feats in the snow.

"Good," said Jean-Pierre, nodding appraisingly as Lisa whooshed into a difficult series of curves. "You are a good pupil. Very supple. You work out, yes? Your muscles are in good shape."

Lisa nodded. "I used to be an aerobics instructor," she told him. "In fact, I was wondering about running an early morning pre-ski class, just to get everyone limbered up."

"Good idea," Jean-Pierre said. "I would like very much to come to one of your classes. Better still –" with a wicked grin that lit up his tanned, healthy face – "better still, I would like you to give me a little personal tuition. I think I could do with some muscle toning. And flexing."

They both laughed, then, and it seemed perfectly natural for him to grasp her hand as he led her up steeper and steeper slopes until they were high into the mountains and far from any other skiers. At last he stopped and turned to her. Lisa's heart was pounding – from the exertion of the climb, but even more from the thrill of being near him, of realizing he still held her hand firmly in his.

There were a few moments of silence, when he looked at her questioningly as though trying to read her mind. Then he said briskly: "Right, now here I am going to teach you a new move, a little tricky but I think you are ready."

For the next hour Lisa could think of nothing but the challenge of learning to master the snow, concentrating hard on the intricate movements Jean-Pierre demonstrated. He was a great teacher – patient but demanding, and very good at inspiring confidence.

"What I am trying to show you," he explained, "is how to deal with difficult terrain, when you will meet bumps and dips. If you learn to do this then we go off piste together."

Lisa couldn't resist giggling at that. "Do you mean you're inviting me out for a drink?"

Jean-Pierre smiled tolerantly. "No, you silly woman. The piste is what we call the official ski runs that are cleared and checked every day. These are very smooth and not dangerous. If you are an advanced skier then you can wander away from the set routes and go off on your own. This, I want to do with you."

The way he said it sent a shiver of expectation

right down Lisa's spine. And then she was back again, practising, as Jean-Pierre taught her, to combine smooth gliding steps with pushes and double pushes so that she would be able to propel herself over mounds and hollows.

"You see, it is like dancing, or like your aerobics," Jean-Pierre explained. "The bumps and dips are like a different rhythm that you must get to know. Imagine your skis are your dancing shoes and the snow is your partner."

Lisa was beginning to feel dizzy – as much from Jean-Pierre's colourful, romantic manner as from the strenuous efforts of the skiing. She stopped and hung her head for a moment, waiting for the feeling to pass.

"Oh, you are tired!" he exclaimed in consternation. "It is my fault. I push you too much. Come, let us go now for something to revive you."

She followed him down the slopes, skimming and bending, speeding up and slowing down, exactly as he did. Soon, they arrived at a tiny wooden chalet, perched picturesquely at the side of a hill. A sign swinging outside showed a sparkling glass and a bottle.

The little alpine café was warm and welcoming, buzzing with conversation and excited tales of bravery on the slopes. Jean-Pierre and Lisa squeezed into a tiny table by the steamy window, and he ordered in German so she had no idea what he'd chosen for her. Soon, two steaming glasses arrived, bubbling with a ferocious-looking red liquid.

"Go on, you will like," Jean-Pierre said firmly.

"It is a special drink of the region. Hot, spicy punch. Very good when you have been out in the snow. It warms you up with a kick." He clinked his glass with hers. "Prosit! Cheers!"

Lisa sipped the drink cautiously. The first sip sent a line of pure fire right down her. The second was just as fiery. Then, gradually, she began to feel a surge of warmth and well-being that seemed to come from right inside her.

"Gosh, Jean-Pierre," she said, her cheeks hot and flushed. "Do you drink a lot of this stuff?"

"Oh, now and again," he replied. "Often, I prefer beer. Or sometimes good strong coffee."

"Just listen to you!" Lisa exclaimed, horrified. "You're addicted to toxins! Don't you know what kind of poisons those drinks contain?" Then she stopped herself, and smiled. He raised his eyebrows, saying nothing.

"Sorry," she mumbled. "Very bad manners, and it's none of my business. I really must stop interfering like this. It's a dangerous sign."

Jean-Pierre looked interested. "What do you mean?"

But Lisa had no intention of letting him know that fussing over a man's diet was her way of showing that she was interested in him. After all, he was just a friendly ski instructor, wasn't he? It wasn't as if things were likely to go any further than that.

4

The Alpine Bar was packed with jostling, shouting, laughing holiday-makers, fresh-faced and happy after their first day on the slopes. Rachel and Lisa sat together at one end of a long trestle table, sipping white wine and soda. Lisa had just given Rachel a fairly accurate version of her afternoon with Jean-Pierre. Which meant that she stuck carefully to the facts, avoiding the feelings.

"So, are you going to tell Alex about him?" asked Rachel, who wasn't fooled for a minute.

"Tell Alex what?" Lisa demanded indignantly. "I told you – nothing happened. He's just a friendly guy who likes teaching people to ski." Rachel said nothing, just looked levelly at her as only Rachel could. They just knew each other too well, Lisa reflected ruefully.

"OK, I admit it, it was exciting," she said eventually, holding up her hands in defeat. "He's really attractive and fun to be with. But that still doesn't mean anything happened. Anyway," she sniffed. "Just because I'm going out with Alex doesn't mean I can't have a bit of fun occasionally, does it? I'm sure he is." Determined to change the subject, she added: "How was your afternoon?"

Rachel frowned. "Not bad to start with. I tried out the slopes with that girl Tammy from Conquest and we had fun. But it was all downhill after that." She paused while Lisa giggled.

"I mean, things started to go wrong," Rachel explained. "The whingeing housewife from Cheam has really got it in for me now because I've given her blisters."

Lisa looked blank. "I mean Janet Maple, Mrs Miserable," Rachel went on glumly. "Her ski boots were too small and she blames me. Funny thing is," she looked thoughtful. "I'm sure they were the right size when we tried them. She was convinced I'd picked up a different pair, with yellow instead of red stitching. Now I come to think about it she could be right about the colour, even though I don't remember putting them down."

She turned to Gudrun, who was sitting at the same table coolly sipping iced water. "Gudrun, you were right next to me this morning. I couldn't have got the shoes mixed up, could I?"

"It is very important that the ski shoes fit exactly," Gudrun answered annoyingly. "So – I would never make such a mistake. But you might, if you do not know so much about skiing."

Rachel glared at her, furious. "Oh, thanks a lot. So nice to have supportive colleagues. Remind me to be there next time you're in an avalanche and I'll be sure to walk away and leave you to it."

Gudrun looked amused. "Rachel, I do not wish to offend you. You are maybe too – too sensitive. I am sure you do not make mix-ups. There. Forgive me?"

Always quick to recover from her outbursts, Rachel grinned at her and Lisa looked relieved. "But whether or not it was my fault, Janet blames me," she carried on. "And she's the most awful sulker. She wouldn't come out tonight because she said her feet were hurting too much. But honestly, they were only tiny blisters."

"How many?" Lisa wanted to know.

"Four," admitted Rachel. "But tiny. I think she's putting it on. And I'm just wondering whether he's got the same idea."

She was looking over Lisa's shoulder at Janet's husband Sean, who was sitting rather gloomily with his friends Mike and Laura, drinking from a pitcher of beer. They seemed to be trying to cheer him up but he just gulped from his tankard from time to time, staring darkly at the floor.

"Oh my God, just look at love's young dream," a spiky voice behind her exclaimed. She turned in time to see Jonquil, dressed from head to toe in an elaborate silk concoction that made her look as though she was covered in peacock feathers. Her jet black hair shone in the dim lights of the bar, her scarlet lipstick making her words somehow seem even more cutting.

She was nodding towards a little alcove where Brett and Nina sat face to face, hands clasped, staring into each other's eyes.

"So very sweet, isn't it?" snarled Jonquil. Her companion, Tommy, shrugged.

"I don't know why she gets so worked up about it," he said to Rachel. "Lucky old Brett, that's what I say."

Jonquil snorted. "Isn't it amazing how men stick together!" she remarked. Then she moved her head closer to Rachel's and said confidingly: "My brother is making a complete donkey of himself, don't you think? Poor thing, it's his mid-life crisis. His wife left him a few months ago, and then he started carrying on with Sweet Valley High over there. So we get landed with the under age Sex Queen for two weeks, holed up together in our little wooden shack."

She must have noticed Rachel's look of annoyance, because she quickly added: "No offence meant, dear, but ski chalet life is hardly my style."

"So why did you choose this holiday?" Rachel asked. She found herself staring with fascination at Jonquil's necklace – a shimmering string of silver snowflakes, each one slightly different in design.

"Well, it's not exactly a holiday," Jonquil explained. "Tommy here – he's my business partner – he discovered that there are some very good outlets for my work in this part of Austria. Lots of little shops where tourists like to buy their souvenirs also stock some quality pieces. So we thought we'd come along and try and do a little business. And because my brother Brett was having a difficult time with his marriage, we asked them to join us and have a little fun at the same time. We thought it might get them back together again. But Cerise refused point blank to come, and this is what we got instead." She shuddered. "It's like being landed with some ghastly stepdaughter."

Rachel laughed. "Oh, come on, she's not that bad. And she's not that young either, is she?"

"Nineteen – just a child!" Jonquil wailed. "Can you imagine having to spend whole evenings with a teenager?"

"Easily," Rachel said simply. "I'm nineteen, too." She enjoyed watching Jonquil's look of incredulity for a moment or two. Then she added: "By the way, I love the snowflakes. I'm sure loads of people will want to buy those."

"Oh, well, thank you – but these are from my most exclusive range," Jonquil said, pleased. "But I've plenty of other designs. While I'm on the slopes during the day, Tommy is going to be setting up appointments with buyers, so we've brought quite a few samples. If you'd like to see some I'd be more than happy to show you."

"Oh, I'd love to!" said Rachel warmly. "If you don't think I'm too young for them, of course."

At that moment, Tammy Thorn burst through the door and bounced over to Rachel and Lisa. "Mind if I join you?" she asked. When she was settled at their table with her drink, she looked round and said, trying to sound casual: "Where's Jason tonight?"

"Oh, he'll be here soon," said Rachel. Lisa noticed Tammy's crestfallen face.

"Rachel's right, he'll turn up. And while you're waiting, why not meet my chalet group? Ten young people, all friends, and none of them couples."

"You lucky thing," said Tammy. "My hotel is meant to be for families. Some nights we even have babysitting duties. The best social life I'm likely to see is helping some New Man change his kid's nappy."

Lisa immediately dragged Tammy over to another table where her wild group were all shrieking with laughter. They made room for Lisa and Tammy, who were soon joining in the fun.

Soon after that, the lights were dimmed, somehow some space was made in the middle of the floor, and people began to dance. Brett and Nina were among the first, locked so close together they were barely dancing at all. Then, one of the boys from Lisa's table grabbed Tammy and pulled her on to the floor, and another followed with Lisa. Soon, the whole area was packed with dancing, swaying couples.

It was then that Jason arrived, and flopped down next to Rachel. "Gosh, have I missed much?" he asked, looking embarrassed. "I fell asleep."

"Too much exertion on the slopes this afternoon?" asked Rachel.

"More likely too much exertion in the kitchen," he grinned. "I just pulled off the most magnificent daube."

"Sounds like a skiing injury," said Rachel, unimpressed. "So what is it?"

"A rich, wine-based, strong, saucy beef stew," said Jason. "And it was perfect. What did you cook?"

"Oh, I didn't," Rachel replied. "I've got Heidi, you see. As well as being a perfect human being who is able to do all the things I hate doing, she's quite happy to cook dinner most of the time. So we had stew as well, and for all I know it could easily have been a daube."

But Jason wasn't really listening to her. He was staring hungrily at Gudrun, who still sat coolly sipping her drink, saying nothing. "Dance, Gudrun?" he burst out finally.

Gudrun turned her eyes slowly towards him and paused for a moment. Then she shrugged her wide, bony shoulders and gave a tiny toss of her head. "OK," she said shortly, got up, and followed him to the dance floor.

Jason was ecstatic. To him, Gudrun was the most exotic and alluring woman he had ever seen. He loved her tall, statuesque figure, her blonde good looks, and her quiet confidence. From the minute he'd set eyes on her he had wanted her. But he liked to think of himself as down to earth, realistic – which made him wonder what a girl like Gudrun could ever see in an ordinary sort of bloke like himself.

It was a slow number, thank goodness, so he had every excuse to take Gudrun in his arms and hold her close. She felt light, moving gracefully across the floor, responding effortlessly to his anxious, faltering steps.

"You're a wonderful dancer," he said, wishing he could think of something more original.

"I had lessons as a girl," Gudrun said. She never seemed to be embarrassed by praise – rather, she expected it.

"You seem to have had lessons in practically everything," he said.

"Yes," she answered simply. "I like to do things properly. It seems to me..." She frowned, searching for the right words. "It is like an insult to do something at all, if you don't do it properly. Don't you think?"

Privately, Jason thought she did an awful lot more things than most people – and certainly far more than him. But he nodded eagerly.

"That's exactly how I feel about cooking," he said. "I love doing it, but the best thing is getting it right, turning the raw ingredients into something different. Sometimes I think I'm making the food taste the way it really wanted to taste in the first place. Do you know what I mean?"

Gudrun's eyes flickered with interest. *Great!* thought Jason. *A response at last – even if it is a very slight response.*

"I, too, feel this way about cooking. Tell me, Jason, which ingredient most of all do you think you are liberating in this way?"

Jason thought quickly. "Tomatoes," he replied. He knew a great recipe for a tomato and onion tart that was very long and complicated. It could take hours to demonstrate it to someone. "I'll show you my secret recipe, if you like?" he said casually.

"I should like that," Gudrun answered graciously. "And I, in return, will show you my speciality. Chocolate ice cake."

Jason was so entranced by Gudrun, so elated with his success, that he didn't even notice Tammy, right beside him. She was dancing with another of Lisa's group – a hearty young guy who was trying to make conversation. But Tammy wasn't listening. She was staring at Jason and Gudrun, her eyes filled with hurt.

"He's not interested in me at all, let's face it," she confided to Rachel as she sat down next to her a little later. "Why do I always attract the rats, and never the nice guys? Do you think it's because I'm a Gemini? We're prone to trouble, you know."

Rachel gave her hand a squeeze. "Come on, Tammy. It's nothing to do with star signs. You know as well as I do that once you attract a nice guy he's quite likely to turn into a rat. It just depends how you look at them. If I were you, I'd give up on Jason at the moment. But, take a look around. The world is full of nice rats. Even if you're a Gemini. Just take your pick!"

A moment later, rather to her surprise, there was a tap on her shoulder. It was Sean Maple. "Fancy a dance?" he asked shyly.

She smiled, then turned to Tammy. "What did I tell you?" she whispered.

Rachel wondered whether Mike and Laura had persuaded him to approach her. They probably thought he needed to have some fun – and she was a safe enough choice. "How's Janet?" she asked brightly as they began to dance.

"Not so great, really," he answered shortly, as if he didn't really want to talk about it. Then, moments later, he seemed to change his mind, and from then on there was no stopping him.

"I know she's not faking it or anything," he began loyally. "She really has got these awful blisters and I'm sure they're very painful. But she sort of seems to give in so easily. She could have come out tonight if she wanted to, but..."

"Perhaps she doesn't want to," suggested Rachel gently. "Why would that be, do you think? She does seem rather ... unhappy."

Sean nodded miserably. "Well, we've been going through a bit of a bad patch. We've been married for four years but this last year we've seemed to do nothing but row all the time. She's dead possessive, you see. She always accuses me of getting off with other people, or fancying other people, or liking people more than I like her."

"And do you?" Rachel was starting to think she could make a living doing this.

"No – I mean, yes..." Sean looked confused. "Look, I love her. I really do. But that doesn't mean I can't talk to anyone but her, does it? She's jealous of the girls at work. She's jealous of my friends. She's even jealous of my mother, and it really gets me down. It's not as if anyone's a threat to her. She's my wife for heaven's sake!"

"Well, she may not feel that way," Rachel said wisely. "Have you ever wondered why she's so possessive? Are you a bit of a flirt, maybe?"

Sean shook his head. "No, I don't think I am. The problem is just Janet. She's very insecure. Maybe it's because – well, my mum and dad are quite well off. And they didn't really approve of her. Didn't want us to get married."

"Aha," said Rachel, desperately trying not to imitate Oprah Winfrey. "So it's your mother who makes her feel insecure. Which is why she's jealous of your mother."

"Maybe, I dunno," muttered Sean, embarrassed. Then he launched on: "Well, maybe there is some truth in that. Janet is really uptight about not knowing how to behave. You know, what to order in restaurants and things. I don't care about things like that. I love her for what she is. But she just gets more and more kind of awkward. She's always dropping things and knocking into things and having accidents."

"Which you find irritating?" suggested Rachel.

"Well, sometimes," admitted Sean. "But only because she gets so upset and then things go wrong and she sort of retreats. So that's why we've come on holiday. To try and have some fun – repair some of the damage."

"So – how did Janet feel about Mike and Laura coming along?" Rachel probed.

Sean winced. "Yeah, spot on. It's not ideal. But Mike's my best friend. We get on fine. He and Laura want to help us get our marriage straight."

"But maybe Janet sees them as the enemy," suggested Rachel, feeling really pleased with herself. If she kept going at this, maybe Janet would forgive her for the blisters. "Do you think Janet might be jealous of them, too?"

Sean thought for a moment, then nodded. "So what can I do?"

The music had changed to a slower tempo, so that now they were dancing cheek to cheek. "Tell you what I think you should do," Rachel murmured in his ear. "Take her off for a day, or an evening. Just the two of you. Show her you want to be with her."

"OK," Sean agreed. "I'll give it a try. I hadn't really seen it that way before." Then he looked up and his face froze. Rachel followed his gaze. Standing in the entrance to the bar, staring straight at them, was Janet. She was very pale, and looked both angry and distraught. After a long, agonized moment, she turned on her heel and left the bar, Sean scurrying after her, helplessly calling her name.

5

"What's half a kilo in pounds?" frowned Rachel, peering anxiously at the huge recipe book.

"Hang on, I'm just working it out," muttered Lisa. She chewed her pencil, scribbled something, crossed it out, then tried all over again.

"Never mind," said Rachel. "Let's do the simple bits first. Crack six eggs. That's six for your cake and six for mine. Whip with vanilla essence. Should be simple. Oh, whoops, it says you've got to melt the chocolate over a double broiler. Would you know one if you saw one?"

Torn between groaning and giggling, the two girls were attempting their first afternoon tea cakes as part of what Marjorie liked to call "those extra little touches".

"Sometimes I think she's a bit touched," said Lisa, creating clouds of fine white dust all round her as she poured flour into the huge, old-fashioned scales. "I mean, as if we didn't have enough to do, she expects us to turn into master bakers."

"It would be such a lovely gesture!" Rachel imitated poor Marjorie, who always tried to make their extra duties sound like extra treats. "And such a wonderful opportunity for you."

Then both girls chorused together, "After all, at Dream Ticket we're just one happy family!" Marjorie said this so often that they'd started keeping a tally.

"She didn't exactly say we had to make them ourselves," Lisa remembered. "They just had to be home-made. But Elsa doesn't like baking."

"Nor does Heidi," Rachel said sadly. "She was really shy for the first couple of days but I think she must have been on an assertiveness course or something. The minute I said the word cake she went all tough and uppity and said she doesn't do cakes and she doesn't do kippers. Well, I told her to relax about the kippers, but I'd kind of appreciate help with the cakes because I haven't the faintest idea how to even begin."

"At least we're in it together," said Lisa. "Hey, look, this is great. The scales are in kilos so I don't have to convert anything after all. Hope they're accurate. Now, what do we do next. Aha – you have to line the tins."

"What do you mean, *I* have to?" Rachel demanded, aghast. "What with? Crayons? Oh, I wish Gudrun or Jason could help!"

"No chance!" scoffed Lisa. "They're too busy creating rival masterpieces."

"Hmm – I'm not so sure about the rival part of

it," mused Rachel. "Did you see them dancing together last night? I think there's something going on between them."

"That would be kind of sweet," said Lisa.

"Yes, I suppose so," Rachel agreed. "Provided she doesn't eat him for dinner."

"Ooh, I wonder what sauce she'd concoct to go with him?" wondered Lisa. "Jason à l'orange? Jason and raspberry coulis? Or how about a nice, traditional Jason and ketchup?"

They were both falling about in hysterics when Nina wandered into the kitchen, looking rather forlorn. "Hi," said Rachel, surprised. "Why aren't you on the slopes today? Are you OK?"

Nina gave a little shrug. "Oh, yeah, I'm fine. It's just that Brett had to do some business up at the hotel – needed to use their computer and fax or something. And frankly, I didn't really fancy tagging along after Cruella de Ville and her loud-mouthed sidekick. So I thought I'd give it a rest for the day."

Rachel didn't comment. It would be very un-professional to make remarks about the clients. But privately she sympathized with Nina. It must be pretty awful stuck all the time with someone who despised you and kept making nasty jibes. And it was probably quite boring, too. Jonquil and Brett were in their thirties – practically middle-aged! No wonder Nina needed a break – and to be with people of her own age.

"Er – you don't know anything about baking, do you?" asked Lisa.

Nina brightened. "Oh, sure – I did it at school.

Hey – can I help?" She looked really pleased at the chance to join them. Lisa and Rachel felt nothing but relief and gratitude.

From then on, baking their cakes was really fun. Nina was a very down-to-earth, practical girl, despite her staggering good looks. She was soon making the others laugh – imitating some of the tourists on the ski slopes, and then had them enthralled, telling them how she'd met Brett back in London, where she'd been working as a secretary with his bank.

"But – doesn't it make a difference that he's so much older?" asked Lisa, curious. "I mean – what do you have in common?"

Nina smiled mischievously. "Oh, we do OK. He's actually very good company – when he's away from his sister. But she's really got it in for me. Like it was my fault he was cheating on his wife. As if I'd have gone out with him if I'd known!"

"You mean, he didn't tell you he was married?" prompted Lisa.

"Let's just say it was something he forgot to mention," said Nina bitterly.

"So do you still trust him?" asked Rachel, fascinated. "Now that you know?"

"Trust doesn't come into it," Nina said. "I'm kind of in too deep now. I suppose I'm just the gullible type. Now then, who's going to beat this chocolate yuck in the blender. Lisa? Hey, Lisa!"

In her enthusiasm Lisa had switched on the blender without securing the lid. It flew off, and thick chocolate sauce spattered everywhere.

"What's going on?" demanded an astonished

voice in the doorway. It was Janet, sporting a pronounced limp and a very red face.

"Janet!" Rachel exclaimed. "Yet another skier refusing to ski. You went yesterday, didn't you? So what happened today?"

"Oh, I didn't really feel up to it today," Janet sniffed. "I think I must have overdone it the other day because my left foot really hurts now, and besides, I got terribly sunburnt. You wouldn't think you could, up there in the snow."

Rachel kept quiet, not wanting to remind Janet that she'd definitely warned everyone about the dangers of the bright sunlight in the mountains. She'd been treating her very carefully ever since Janet had glimpsed her dancing with Sean two evenings before, and had stormed off in a rage. "Well, now that you're here, what do you know about kitchens?"

To her amazement Janet brightened considerably. "Ah, now that's something I can do," she announced. "Move over, I'll deal with this." So Rachel and Lisa looked on, bemused, as Janet briskly got to work cleaning up the devastation they'd created in the kitchen, and Nina happily mixed up two gigantic chocolate cakes.

Rachel wondered why Janet had really decided against skiing that day. Was she still feeling so insecure with Sean and his friends? She certainly seemed in her element now, bustling round with a mop and bucket.

"So Janet – I bet Sean's missing you today," she tried at last. "Can't be nearly as much fun without you."

Immediately, Janet stiffened and the relaxed look was gone, replaced by one of fury. "Yes, well, you'd know, wouldn't you?" she rasped. "I'd appreciate it if you'd keep your nose out of my affairs – and your hands off my husband, OK?"

"Janet, I'm not the least bit interested in your husband," Rachel called helplessly as Janet flounced out of the room. "And he's not interested in me – or anyone else. I'm sure of it."

Janet poked her head round the door. "Don't you tell me what my own husband is like, thank you very much," she stormed. "You don't know anything."

And she was off, leaving Rachel feeling rather stunned.

"Bit theatrical, isn't she?" remarked Nina calmly, licking her mixing spoon. "Don't worry – she'll get over it. Now, let's get these mixtures into the tins, OK? Rachel, you turn your oven to Mark Four, right?"

As they were spooning the last of the rich, brown mess into the second tin, there was a rap on the door. Gudrun and Jason appeared, looking very pleased with themselves.

"Ah, chocolate cake," commented Gudrun. "Very nice, very – er – traditional. Your English guests, they will like this, I think."

"Oh, and what have you made for your German guests?" asked Rachel.

"Me, I have created a selection of Viennese pastries with iced toppings in the flavours of berries," Gudrun replied smoothly.

"Me, too," Jason chimed in, his face glowing.

49

"Gudrun has shown me one of her secret recipes. And tomorrow I'm going to show her how to do perfect Yorkshire pudding. We just popped round to see if you'd like to come for a swim before teatime."

"No time," said Lisa. "We're just going to put Rachel's cake in the oven, and then we're going next door to do mine. And Nina's going to stay and do the icing for both of us."

They didn't look very heartbroken to discover that it would be just the two of them in the pool. In fact, Jason looked pleased enough to burst.

Rachel quickly popped her cake into the oven and went next door to join Lisa and Nina.

"This is really nice of you, Nina," Rachel told her as they sat drinking coffee round the kitchen table in Lisa's Green Chalet.

"No problem," said Nina. "I'm enjoying myself, if you want to know the truth. I'd forgotten what good clean fun could be like."

They sat and chatted companionably until the timer bleeped on Lisa's oven. Rachel rushed back to her chalet, expecting to be greeted by the delicious aroma of fresh baking. Instead, to her shock, the kitchen was full of smoke and there was an acrid smell of burning. She rushed over to open the oven. The cake was a black, smouldering ruin.

Choking from the fumes, Rachel reached to switch off the oven. She gasped in horror as she saw the number on the dial. Eight. The gas had been set at Mark Eight instead of Mark Four. No wonder the cake had burned to a cinder!

Rachel quickly opened the windows and the front door, to let out the smoke and get some fresh air. How could she have made such a mistake? Or – had someone made it for her?

But there was no time to speculate. She was in trouble. The cold, hungry members of her chalet group would be returning in the next hour – expecting a special tea. Marjorie was counting on her. She'd already said she was coming on one of her inspections that afternoon.

Rachel dashed next door to Lisa – but even Nina couldn't help. "Just give 'em some digestive biscuits from the tuck shop," she advised. "They can be very comforting when you're far from home."

Next, Rachel dashed across the road to the Alpine Centre. There was just a chance that Jason or Gudrun could help out. She bumped into Jason as he was emerging from the lockers. "Any chance that you could spare a few of your super-duper Viennese whatsits?" she begged.

But even good-natured Jason wasn't prepared to part with his masterpieces. "We only just made enough to go round our two chalets," he said. "Sorry, Rachel – bad luck!"

But Rachel was gone before he'd even finished his sentence. She'd had one last idea. She may not be able to provide Viennese pastries, she thought, but how about Danish ones?

She raced down the narrow, icy streets to the town's tiny central square, very nearly toppling into lamp posts and trees as she slithered down the slippery, hilly paths. At last, she caught sight of the wooden sign, welcoming her to Karl's Place. She flung herself through the door, panting so hard she could barely speak.

Karl was alone in the little shop. He looked delighted to see her. "Ah, my English friend," he greeted her. "You have come to the best place in town to sample my unbeatable Kaffee und Küchen – coffee and cakes."

"Er, no – not exactly," Rachel said anxiously, then began to explain her problem.

He stood behind the counter patiently, eyeing her with quiet amusement as she recounted her sorry tale. "So," she finished desperately. "I was just wondering – can you help me at all? I mean, I'd like to buy some pastries. And – er – it would help a lot if they looked home-made."

"Do not worry, your troubles are over," Karl said grandly. "Now all my pastries, of course, are very first rate, all home baked. But today I have something special. Something I think you will like." He disappeared for a few moments into the back of the shop, and emerged triumphantly with two magnificent ring cakes, each with a hole in the middle. One was a plain cake, dusted with fine sugar, the other chocolate. Both had been moulded all round with ripples. They were still hot from the oven. Rachel gazed at them, thinking they were the most beautiful sight she'd ever encountered. She reached out for them. But Karl teasingly snatched them back.

"Just one thing," he said nonchalantly. "One – what do you call it? One condition. I give you these cakes – and you come out with me on a date, yes?"

"But that's blackmail!" protested Rachel.

"Yes," said Karl simply.

Rachel thought about it hard. For about a second. Then she said: "Done! How much do I owe you?"

"Nothing," Karl said. "It is a gift. It is my pleasure. And next time, it will be your turn to do the favour, yes?"

But Rachel was by now out of the door, racing up the hill to the Dream Ticket chalets.

By the time her group were crowding into the dining room, tea was ready to be poured, the table was laid, and the two cakes sat on silver plates in pride of place.

Rachel stood smiling beatifically, nodding at everyone's exclamations and compliments. Inside, though, she was in turmoil. She'd got away with it – just about! But had someone deliberately sabotaged her? If so, who?

Her eyes lit on Janet, who was looking strained as Sean, Mike and Laura regaled her with a lively account of their day. An awful suspicion began to creep over her. After all, Janet had been so hostile today, so convinced that Rachel was a rival, trying to steal her husband away. And Janet had been in the chalet all afternoon, while Rachel had been with Lisa. She'd had every opportunity to carry out the sabotage. But would she really do something so petty and spiteful?

For the time being, all Rachel could do was continue to pour the tea, smile and nod, and try to hide the growing sense of panic that things, somehow, were veering out of control.

6

The early evening sun was beating down on the parched sand. Dotted along the beach were tall palm trees silhouetted against the deepening yellow of the sky, and the azure waters of the sea. It was heaven, pure heaven, thought Alex, sitting at a little table at a waterfront café, sipping his Coke. Here he was in mid-December, when England would be shrouded in drizzle and grey, damp skies – wearing only swimming trunks and a T-shirt, and basking in this dazzling view of paradise. Talk about striking lucky!

But right then, Alex didn't feel all that lucky. He sighed, his troubled eyes furrowed. Something wasn't right, he was sure. He'd just spoken to Lisa, long-distance to Austria. He'd been so excited that he couldn't wait to tell her the news.

"Lisa – Lisa, are you there? It's me, Alex."

"Oh, hi – how are you?" She sounded pleased enough to hear from him – but not pleased enough for Alex. Why wasn't she shrieking his name?

"Oh, fine. I'm great. It's hot, beautiful, food's wonderful. Best hamburgers I've ever tasted."

"Oh, that's nice," replied Lisa. Alex felt crestfallen. Normally he only had to say the word hamburger for Lisa to launch into one of her frenzied lectures about E-numbers and saturated fats and the bits of cows that didn't bear thinking about. So what had got into her?

"Listen, I'm just ringing to say I can make it over for Christmas," Alex told her. "I've done a deal – I can come for a week, starting next Thursday on Christmas Eve. And I don't have to be back until 2 January, so we can bring in the New Year together."

"Oh, Alex, that's fantastic!" enthused Lisa. "I can't wait – there's so much to tell you. But Alex, are you sure you're going to have the right clothes? Did you pack anything suitable for skiing along with all those Hawaiian shirts and surfing shorts?"

She sounded genuine enough, he had to admit that. It was typical of Lisa to start fretting about whether he'd be warm enough, when he was only interested in being with her again, holding her in his arms, feeling her sensational, lithe body pressed against his...

But Alex was still sure there was something different about her. She sounded more distant, more detached somehow. "Lisa, are you sure you want me to come?"

There was a pause. Only a fragment of a pause. No more than a couple of seconds before she answered, "Of course I do, silly. I'm dying to see you. What's the problem? Too many girls chasing you round the pool?"

Alex laughed, knowing that she was teasing him. "No one as wonderful as you," he said tenderly. "Lisa – I love you. I want you so much I can almost feel your breath, coming over the phone line. It's making me feel all hot and weak. I'm not sure if I can wait a whole week. But … you do love me, don't you?"

"Course I do," she answered quickly. Too quickly, he thought anxiously. Maybe she was just trying to get rid of him. "Listen, Alex, I'm really excited, but I've gotta go now. It's time for my skiing lesson. See you soon. Love ya!"

And she was gone. Alex took another sip of his Coke. It tasted strangely flat and unexciting. He missed having Lisa shouting at him to stop consuming all that liquid tooth decay. Without her, nothing tasted quite so exciting.

"Hey, Alex," called a group of girls from the beach. "We're going to rent some pedalos. Fancy coming with us?" He looked up. There were four of them – all incredibly sexy, and all very friendly. Dream Ticket girls always loved Alex.

But he smiled sadly and shook his head. He didn't feel like having fun with these girls right then. However lovely they were, they weren't Lisa. He sat brooding for a while. The next time he looked up he could see the girls pedalling their boat into the distant horizon, could hear their distant shrieks of laughter. One of them had stripped off her T-shirt to reveal the tiniest of bikinis, before diving off the side into the surf-topped waves.

"Mad," Alex muttered to himself. "I must be barmy. What other bloke would land a job like this, in a place like this, surrounded by women like this – and not enjoy it?" But he couldn't help it. His thoughts now were all for Lisa. And no matter how he tried to reason with himself, he couldn't shake off the feeling that he might be losing her.

"See you soon. Love ya!" Lisa said quickly, making two quick kissy noises into the phone before putting down the receiver. Then she rushed back into the bedroom of the apartment she shared with Rachel, pulled on boots, scarf and hat, and rushed out of the door, grabbing her skis as she went.

She was late. Jean-Pierre would be stamping impatiently up on the high slopes, occasionally swooping into elegant geometric shapes in the deep snow with increasing speed. Jean-Pierre was a man of action. He didn't like to be kept waiting.

This was Lisa's third private lesson since that first, memorable afternoon. Each time, Jean-Pierre urged her into more intricate and daring manoeuvres. And each time, too, he would lead her higher and higher into the mountains, and further away from all the other skiers.

As Lisa mounted the special T-bar lift and felt herself being pulled gently up yet another slope, she barely had time to reflect on her conversation just a little while earlier with Alex. Part of her was really glad that he would be coming. She was truly fond of him and missed him. But another, wilder part of her just wanted to continue these adventures in the mountains with Jean-Pierre – the excitement of being with this strong, athletic, totally self-sufficient man, and the tantalizing mystery of never quite knowing what would happen.

Not that anything much had happened yet. Jean-Pierre was such a dedicated teacher that Lisa wondered whether he'd be impatient at the thought of anything as ordinary as romance – unless it was the romance of the mountains, the peaks and slopes, the never-ending attraction of the unpredictable, beautiful, treacherous snow. So he'd often stand very close to her, think nothing of wrapping his arms tight round her while showing her a new technique, or pulling her to her feet after a fall. But that was it. He'd never kissed her, even though Lisa was sometimes almost breathless with anticipation, just in case...

Today, though, it was different. She could feel it from the moment they reached the top of the T-bar line and found themselves alone in a very remote part of the mountain. "Today, I think you are ready," he announced solemnly. Lisa nearly squeaked she was so startled. "Today, we are going to begin to ski off piste, yes?"

Oh, so that's what he thought she was ready for? For a moment, she felt a pang of disappointment, but soon, she was caught up in the magic of the quiet, still beauty of the alpine scene, and the thrill of becoming part of it.

"Now, the snow here is a little different," Jean-Pierre was explaining carefully. "It is softer, more like powder, because it is very fresh. You must do the short swinging that I have been showing you so you can have more control."

He moved lightly towards her and stood behind her, one arm circled a little away from her right side. "Let me feel you lean your weight here," he said. Then he did the same with his left arm. "And here. That's right. Show me how you are going to use your body to steer the snow. Good, now I want to feel how you make the rhythm."

Surely now, thought Lisa, now he would turn her with those strong, powerful arms, pull her towards him, crush her against his chest. But he didn't. He just murmured: "Good, very good," and gently pushed her down the slope, calling after her: "Now you try it alone – swing, Lisa, swing through the snow!"

And she was off, skimming lightly in snake-like curves through the soft, powdery snow, bending into the turns this way and that as she gathered speed until she felt as though she was floating. It was the most exquisite feeling of freedom, the wind stroking her cheeks, the sun warming her back, and the snow welcoming her like a lover as she surfed down the steep, majestic mountainside.

It seemed like for ever that she and Jean-Pierre were together, alone on that solitary slope. At least, she wished it would go on for ever. It was as though she was caught up in a dream – in a time and landscape of their own, with the real world far, far away. And even when they descended back down the T-bar and then down another lift to their own little café, she still didn't feel she'd quite woken up.

As they left the café and were about to ski down the final slope back to Edelweiss, he suddenly caught her hand and stopped walking. "You are quite special, Lisa," he said. "Very – how you say it – plucky. And very sexy." Then slowly, gently, he pulled her towards him and bent his face to hers until their lips touched. A flame darted through her.

Then, at last, he was kissing her properly, his mouth bruising hers in a long, hungry embrace. Then, finally, it was Lisa who pulled away from him in dismay and confusion. "I – I'm sorry," she said in a rush. "But you see, I have a boyfriend."

Jean-Pierre's eyes were smouldering still. He said nothing, just stared at her for a few seconds. Then his handsome face creased into smiles.

"Yes, me too. I have a girlfriend. Believe me, Lisa, I have wanted to do this before now, all the time. I thought maybe she would not like very much. But now I think, well, she is far away. And so – there is no harm, I believe…"

"But you don't understand," Lisa protested. "He'll be here soon. He's coming to see me next week, for Christmas."

Jean-Pierre looked unconcerned. "Good. Then we have a whole week to get to know each other. Really well…"

When tea was over later that afternoon, Rachel and Lisa headed straight for the sauna. For a few minutes they lay sprawled on the wooden slats, breathing in the heady scent of eucalyptus rising from the glowing coals. But gradually Lisa became aware that Rachel was unusually subdued.

"What's up, Rach?" she asked solicitously. "You're awfully quiet today."

Rachel was feeling so low that she couldn't even look at Lisa. But she was longing to pour out her heart to her friend. So she wriggled on to her back until she was lying flat out, sweating in the intense heat. Then she began to talk.

"I don't know, Lisa... Everything seems to be going wrong for me at the moment. Today started badly because I got a letter from Jack."

"But that's good, isn't it?" Lisa put in.

"Oh, it was fine. Except that he definitely can't come here for Christmas. He says he's much too busy, loads of last-minute bookings at his resort, and lots of fiddly changes. I'm just wondering if it's all just one big excuse..."

"Don't be daft!" scoffed Lisa. "Jack's crazy about you, you know he is."

"Yeah, maybe," said Rachel dully. "Anyway, how about Alex? Is he going to be able to make it?"

Lisa felt a sudden surge of guilt, remembering that heady kiss with Jean-Pierre in the mountains. How could she be behaving that way with him, when Alex would be there in just a few days? She couldn't imagine Rachel doing anything like that. And poor Rachel wouldn't even be seeing Jack at Christmas...

"But that's not all," Rachel was saying miserably. And then, in a rush, out came her story about the burnt cake – how she was becoming convinced that someone had turned up the gas deliberately to land her in trouble.

"But why?" Lisa interrupted. "Why should anyone have it in for you?"

"That's what I keep wondering," said Rachel. "But you know that cake business happened very soon after Janet saw me dancing with Sean. You saw her in the kitchen yesterday – she really thinks there's something going on between us, no matter what I say. And she was there, alone in the chalet while I was next door with you. So maybe she was trying to get back at me. And there was that other time, too. The first day, when she accused me of swapping her boots. I've started to wonder whether she did that herself, to get at me."

"Now you really are being daft. That was before she saw you with Sean, so she wouldn't have had any reason to get at you, would she?" Lisa reasoned.

"Suppose not," said Rachel. "But I still think she could have turned up the oven. And who knows what she'll try next?"

Lisa thought for a minute. "You know what I think? I think you're upset, because you're used to doing everything right and you can't bear it if anything goes wrong. Look, Rachel – everybody makes mistakes sometimes. Even you. So join the rest of the world and live with it, and stop being so paranoid."

Rachel got up, suddenly feeling much too hot. "Maybe you're right. I do hate being clumsy at skiing, and I really hate cooking! But I'm still not sure… I think I need a swim."

She left the sauna and dived straight into the pool, gasping for a few moments at the shock of the cold water, and then beginning to enjoy the sensation as she made her way strongly down one length. Soon Lisa joined her and they were splashing happily together when Jason appeared, fully dressed, but peering all round as though he was looking for something.

"Hey, Rachel," he called. "You haven't seen my key-ring, have you? It's that special silver one, with the ace of hearts on it. I just wondered because I'm sure I had it here yesterday. Remember when you came to ask about those pastries at the locker room? I could have sworn I had it with me..."

"Oh, great!" stormed Rachel, swinging up the ladder at the end of the pool. "Just great! As if everything else wasn't enough, now you're accusing me of stealing your key-ring! That's just wonderful!"

"No, I wasn't!" protested Jason mildly. "Honestly, Rachel, of course I wasn't. It's just that you were here when I had it and I thought maybe..."

"You thought maybe I'd seen it hanging out of your locker and thought, that's a nice key-ring, I think I'll take it. Or maybe you thought I snuck it out of your pocket when you weren't looking!"

"Don't be daft, Rachel," Lisa said, alarmed. "No one could possibly think that."

"Course not," added Jason, clearly upset.

"OK," muttered Rachel. "So you weren't accusing me. But listen – something strange is going on. Who knows, maybe someone took the key-ring just to get at me!"

"Now that is paranoid!" said Lisa and Jason both together.

"You could be right," said Rachel unhappily. "But it's certainly how it's beginning to feel to me." And with that she stormed off to the changing room.

Jason and Lisa gazed at each other helplessly. Lisa could see that Jason was feeling responsible for upsetting Rachel, so she linked her arm in his.

"Come on, cheer up," she said. "It's not your fault. Why don't I help you look for the key-ring? Maybe it's over by the counter where the clean towels are kept?"

As they sauntered arm in arm towards the reception bar, they didn't notice that Gudrun had appeared in the doorway. In fact, they weren't aware of her presence until she'd silently followed them right round the pool and joined them at the desk.

"So are you going to say hi?" she asked in her deep voice. Lisa gasped and turned round.

"Oh, Gudrun, you gave me a shock!" she gasped. "We – er, Jason and I – were just looking for his key-ring. You know, that really pretty one with the ace of hearts on it."

"Ah, I see," said Gudrun. "Yes, I remember it, Jason. Careless of you to lose it. But how nice that Lisa is helping you to search for it. I will see you later, yes?"

She stalked off with Jason running after her, calling out, "Gudrun! Gudrun, wait for me!" Lisa shrugged, and carried on searching for the missing key-ring. Alone.

7

Rachel sat on the bed in Jonquil's room, her eyes wide with wonder at the dazzling array being displayed before her. There were more silver snowflake sets of necklaces and earrings; brightly-coloured combinations of semi-precious jewels; brooches worked into the shapes of animals; and, best of all, a series based on music: saxophone earrings; brooches made up of complete jazz bands and string quartets; and a little set of silver pins, each a tiny musical instrument.

As Rachel squawked and exclaimed with pleasure, Jonquil's normally rather angular, haughty face softened with pleasure, her eyes for once animated with genuine interest. She may be a terrible snob and horrible to Nina, Rachel thought to herself, but she's really talented. Now that we're on her territory, looking at her work, I almost like her...

"You see, I like to work in themes," Jonquil

explained. "Sometimes I travel to different parts of the world to pick up ideas. These –" she indicated a set of bright turquoise designs set in dark, heavy silver – "These were inspired by a trip to Mexico. The Aztecs always work in turquoise and no one does it better than they do."

"What about the musical theme?" asked Rachel.

Jonquil laughed, a sad little laugh. "Oh, that was an affair that didn't work out. I fell in love with a musician – something I advise you never to do."

She scrabbled in yet another box and brought out something wrapped in tissue paper. "This is a part of that collection, but I've a feeling I might have trouble selling it, don't you?"

She unwrapped a delicately-worked little brooch, so intricate it looked as if it had been woven in silver lace. Rachel looked closely and saw that it was a spider playing a cello, its legs wound round the instrument as if it were a man's hands round a woman's waist. With it were two perfect earrings in the shape of cellos, but with snakes coiled round them.

"They're – they're beautiful," Rachel said at last. "But they're more like sculptures than pieces of jewellery. There's so much passion in them."

Jonquil gave her a long, intense look – then laughed a brittle little laugh. "Well, that's certainly true. Actually, I wasn't even going to try to interest anyone in these. But Tommy and I are meeting a rather special client, the day after Christmas. He owns some small galleries in Switzerland and Austria specializing in designer jewellery. So who knows? Maybe these pieces will appeal to him." She tucked the little box lovingly under her pillow. "Now, why don't I show you my latest ideas. Right now I'm working mainly in jet..."

And she started showing Rachel the strings of glossy black stones she was working into necklaces.

Rachel was so engrossed in looking at the jewellery that she was shocked to realize that nearly an hour had gone by. It was Wednesday, and there were no skiing lessons that morning, so she was meant to be around in case her group needed her.

"Oh, don't worry about them," Jonquil advised her languidly. "They'll go and play in the snow and be quite happy without you."

Rachel was amused. "Don't you fancy playing in the snow yourself, then?"

"A little skiing in the morning is quite enough for me," said Jonquil. "Too much fresh air can play havoc with the complexion. And besides, Tommy and I have work to do."

When Rachel got back to the apartment at about twelve o'clock Lisa was getting bundled up and ready to leave. "Oh, hi Rachel, fancy coming on an adventure?"

"What sort of adventure?" Rachel wanted to know.

"Well, as it's a free afternoon, my chalet group has asked me to go skiing with them. They want to try somewhere a bit different, so I said I'd take them up that other ski lift, you know, the one that goes to the Santa Claus run."

Rachel gasped in horror. "You! You're taking them up there! You're crazy, Lisa!"

Lisa looked defiant. "I don't see why," she argued. "I've been up there loads of times with Jean-Pierre, and I know Gudrun's taken her group there because she told me. And if she can do it I can. Besides, they asked me – and I'm only trying to please them. Don't look so horrified, Rachel – it's not nearly as steep as it looks. Coming?"

Rachel shook her head. "Be careful!" she called rather feebly, as Lisa rushed out and banged the door. "Bye," she added, even though no one could hear her.

Lisa was feeling exuberant as she led her laughing, chattering chalet group up the mountain. There was much hilarity when it came to riding the T-bar lifts. Everyone seemed to want her help, everyone was looking to her to show them the way. And as she'd done this very route several times with Jean-Pierre, she was confident that she knew all there was to know about it.

She remembered the last time he'd taken her to this remote little run. "This pass," he'd told her then, "they call it the Santa Claus, I think because the children of the village believe that this is where Santa Claus and his reindeer come from. But also because many of the Austrian passes are named after Saints. And me, now, I have another reason for the name."

Lisa's face glowed with excitement as she remembered how he'd crushed her in his arms, kissed her hungrily, and murmured: "You are my

Christmas angel. My best, most beautiful..." He'd given her one of his deep, searching looks, then added quietly, passionately: "And I think you are not just a decoration on a tree, Lisa. Very soon, you are going to give yourself to me..."

But as they reached the top of the slope, Lisa forced herself to put aside her enticing memories. There was work to be done. "Right, just follow me," she instructed the group confidently. "As you know, the slopes on the piste are always flagged so that you know where you are and what the skiing conditions are like. You'll see the usual coloured markers – blue for easy slopes, red for medium and black for the most difficult. We'll stick to blue, shall we?"

"But Lisa," interrupted Cindy, one of the livelier girls. "It all looks difficult to me. I didn't realize it would be like this. Look, we're the only ones up here."

"Don't be such a baby!" scoffed a couple of the boys. "We'll be OK, won't we, Lisa?"

Lisa felt a momentary misgiving. Dream Ticket didn't explicitly forbid the reps from conducting little outings on the slopes, but you were supposed to keep within sensible confines. Had she led them too far away from the main slopes? Just because she could handle the runs with Jean-Pierre, it didn't mean she was qualified to lead a whole group of new skiers.

But then she spotted the familiar blue markers in the snow. Great – that meant the slopes would be easy. "Let's just try these easy runs for a bit," she suggested. And soon everyone was swooshing happily down the first part of the run. When they came to a second, much steeper-looking slope, Lisa was relieved that that, too, was flagged with a blue marker.

But wait – something was wrong. There was no doubt about it, this was a far more difficult run. She could feel it as she led the way down. She was having to use all the tactics Jean-Pierre had taught her, to negotiate the steep, uneven curve of the land. Almost at once, she could tell that some of the others were having difficulty.

"Heeey!" yelled a couple of the lads as they careered past her, sticks flailing. "Wow! This is fast!"

Then, inevitably, came a scream. From Cindy. Not expecting such a sharp incline, she'd lost control of her skis and went flying over, landing in a heap in a snow drift.

Feeling distinctly uneasy now, Lisa helped her to her feet. "This doesn't seem right," she told her, worried. "I guess the blue flags mean this is easy if you're incredibly experienced." She turned to the rest of the group, who'd gathered round. "Maybe it's not such a good idea for us to have come so far. Shall I just lead the way down that slope, back to the lifts?"

They nodded, looking a little subdued, even though some of the lads were clearly rather pleased with themselves for managing a steep slope. Well, at least this next one's still blue, Lisa told herself nervously. Even if they seem to have a funny idea about what's easy round here.

The others stood in a cluster, watching, as Lisa

took off. She could tell at once that this slope was even trickier than the last. Suddenly, the ground seemed to drop from beneath her, and she went hurtling down, down, faster and faster, desperately trying to ride the snow and skim over the treacherous holes and bumps.

Then another, even steeper drop, and this time she was completely out of control, racing into the unknown, faster, faster, until suddenly, CRASH! She'd landed hard into something – no, someone. Someone so strong and powerfully built that he'd managed to stem the momentum of her headlong rush. Someone who even now was cradling her against his chest, his arms holding her tight, his face a mask of concern.

"Lisa!" exclaimed Jean-Pierre. "Lisa what are you doing here? These slopes are not for you. You are not ready. And who...?" He looked up at the curious group, still gathered at the top of the slope. "Who are they?"

Lisa, trembling with shock, was practically in tears. "I thought it was safe here," she gulped. "I'd been up the T-bar lift with you. And they wanted to come. They're my chalet group, you see, and they said they'd like to try a different part of the mountain..."

Jean-Pierre looked rather grim. "And you thought you'd like to impress your friends? Lisa, this is no game. These slopes are not for anyone. You have to be an advanced skier, very experienced, to tackle them. Look down there."

Below them was a stunning wilderness of alpine slopes, dotted with snow-covered trees. It looked like a skier's paradise. But Lisa could see what Jean-Pierre was trying to point out: there was nobody there, nobody at all. These slopes were deserted because they were too dangerous for normal holiday-makers.

"But we've been up the lifts before," protested Lisa. "Surely they wouldn't let us up if they thought it was that dangerous."

Jean-Pierre shrugged. "You have authority – you wear the Dream Ticket band. So if anyone saw you they would think you were qualified to lead your party. But maybe no one saw you. Lisa, you didn't go down the right way. You were leading your group down a different route, a much more difficult one, where I have never taken you. It is very, very easy to confuse the way when there is snow."

He shouted to the group: "Please – you wait there. I show you a different way back." As they all trudged after him, Lisa pointed to the flags along the route.

"What I don't understand is why they've put blue markers along here, if it's so dangerous."

Jean-Pierre looked puzzled. "This is not right," he said, his eyes narrowing as he surveyed the flags. "If anything, they should be marked with black. I wonder, has someone been having a joke. Me, I do not think it very funny."

Lisa was worried that Jean-Pierre would be angry with her for leading her group into danger. But he seemed more concerned about the wrong coloured flags. "I must report this," he muttered to himself, as he led her party to safety. "But first, I think, we must cheer up your friends."

Somehow, after they'd taken the lifts down to a more populated part of the mountain, Jean-Pierre organized some skiing games on the more familiar slopes. They did some easy races, and then he invented a kind of follow-my-leader in the snow, with everyone having to imitate madder and madder movements until they were all shrieking with laughter.

As they made their way back down the slope to the village, Lisa and Jean-Pierre slowed down, until they were out of sight of the others.

"Lisa, you did something foolish today," he began.

Lisa flushed. "I know – it was crazy. But I was so sure it would be safe. Honestly, Jean-Pierre, I'm not completely stupid. I'd never have taken them there if I'd realized..."

Jean-Pierre shook his head. "No, listen to me. I wanted to say to you that you were in danger today. I do not like to think what would have happened to you if I had not been there. It made me feel very bad."

He turned to her and slowly took her in his arms. "You see, you matter to me. Very much. I do not like to think of you being harmed."

And then he was kissing her, seriously kissing her, his mouth bruising hers with a hunger and passion that sent her senses reeling. "Be mine, Lisa," he whispered. "I want you so much – so very much."

8

Rachel, meanwhile, had been careering from one disaster to another. As soon as Lisa had banged out of the apartment, Gudrun had appeared. "Oh, Rachel – I have a message for you. Heidi is not able to show up today."

Oh, that's just great, Rachel thought with a sigh. As if I don't have enough to do. Feeling like a martyr, she made her way back to the deserted chalet and half-heartedly began to tidy up. If there was one thing Rachel loathed even more than cooking it was housework, and she bitterly resented having to do it. So she rushed through it as quickly as possible, sweeping the floors, tidying the kitchen and piling books and magazines into fairly neat piles.

Heidi was supposed to clean the bedrooms every day, but Rachel decided that was beyond the call of duty. She just slipped into each one, straightened the duvets and pillows, and left it at that.

As soon as she'd finished she made her way over

to Northern Heights. It was her turn to be on duty – something none of the reps enjoyed very much, because it usually involved them in tedious paperwork, helping with lost traveller's cheques or filling out endless insurance forms. There were always masses of medical claims on skiing holidays, and everyone went to elaborate lengths to get other people to take them on. So far, Rachel had been lucky. But she had a feeling that today was bound to be full of minor irritations.

Her gloomy musings were interrupted by a cheerful "Hi!" from Tammy, who'd just entered the building looking hopeful and enquiring. Rachel had a feeling she knew what was coming next. Sure enough, it did.

"Seen Jason anywhere?" Tammy asked. Before Rachel could even begin to reply she held up her hands in good-humoured defeat. "I know, I know. He's not interested. He's a lost cause. But the trouble is, I *like* lost causes. And besides, I know he and that Gudrun are just not suited."

"How did you work that out?" Rachel asked, laughing.

"Easy," Tammy shrugged. "He's an Aries, she's a Capricorn. Chalk and cheese. Oh, she's very attractive. But it can't work, can it? And not only that – her rising sign is moon-dominant, which obviously explains why she's so cool and unemotional. But Jason's all fire and water, just like me. I'm a Gemini, so we're bound to get on."

As she was chattering, Sean and Janet appeared in the hall, with Mike and Laura trailing behind. They all looked rather disconsolate.

Rachel leaned over the counter of her reception desk. "What's up? You lot look as if the Abominable Snowman has just eaten your snowshoes. Why aren't you out there practising your diagonal side-stepping or something?"

"We decided to have a rest from skiing," explained Mike. "We've been skating instead, on the village lake."

"It was Janet's idea," put in Laura, rather unnecessarily, Rachel thought.

"Well, we go skating a lot at home – I thought it would be fun," Janet defended herself, looking unhappy as usual.

"And it was OK for a while. But some of the village lads starting teasing us," Laura went on. "They threw snowballs and started laughing at us. And Mike tried to stop them so then they threw even bigger snowballs, and it could have turned really nasty."

"But I thought it wouldn't be a good idea to get into a fight," explained Sean.

"And I thought that was pathetic," put in Janet. "I mean, what kind of guys don't even defend their own wives?"

"Yes, well they were quite – well built," said Mike.

Rachel and Tammy glanced at each other and began to laugh – quietly at first, and then more and more helplessly.

Janet looked offended, but the others grinned and eventually started laughing themselves.

"Oh, dear – what am I going to do with you?" Rachel managed to gasp at last. "I could put some of you in the sand pit and the rest in the Wendy House, but, er … they're being used by the Snowball Club at the moment. The one for Under Fives!"

"Let's take you all tobogganing," suggested Tammy. And the moment she and Rachel started to get the toboggans ready, several other people wandering round the centre perked up and said they'd like to come too.

"Just make sure they're in good nick," Tammy warned Rachel, who was busy checking over the first two out of the cupboard. Then her face clouded over as Gudrun appeared, with her troop of very sporty Germans.

"Ah, tobogganing. What fun!" Gudrun remarked pleasantly, as she squeezed past them to where the ski equipment was stored.

"Why not come with us?" suggested Rachel.

"No – no thank you. It is a little too childish, I think, for my party. They are very keen to go exploring. Already this morning we have had some practice on the slopes and now we are planning to ski overland to Mittelhorn for lunch. But first I must find bindings for everyone, to attach the skis to the boots."

Gudrun busied herself with bindings and toe-caps while Rachel and Tammy carefully checked their remaining four toboggans. "Right, those look OK," said Tammy, studiously ignoring Gudrun. "Childish!" she muttered to Rachel. "What a cheek! Doesn't she realize that the Aries man always has a strong childish streak? Just like us Geminis!"

"Hang on a minute," said Rachel. "We're two

short, aren't we?" She counted. "Yes, I'm sure there should be two more."

"Oh, are you looking for those red toboggans?" asked Gudrun casually. "I think they are over in the office. Someone was wanting some yesterday when I was on duty. Foolish, some people. They were English, I think!"

Tammy glowered at her as Rachel rushed over to retrieve the final two sledges.

Tammy's idea turned out to be a great success. The two girls had attracted six more Dream Ticket people, so that there were twelve altogether in their party. They made for the nearest nursery slopes, dragging the toboggans behind them on ropes.

Very soon, all the petty feelings of the day were swept aside, and everyone was shrieking with laughter and excitement as they raced the toboggans down the first, gentle runs. They went in pairs, then in trios, racing men against women, then mixed teams. There were several dramatic spills in the snow, but that just added to the general hilarity.

After a while, Tammy suggested they go up a little higher. "There's a really great run for toboggans over there," she gestured. "Usually it's used for one of the advanced ski groups, but it's wonderful for sledging." They tramped after her, to the top of a hill that glistened invitingly with thick, fresh snow. It looked steeper than the previous runs, but very smooth and deep.

They decided to start by going down one to a sledge. "It's really fast, but easier to control if there's just one person," Tammy explained.

At first, this was a great success. Mike whizzed down the slope and said it was brilliant. Sean followed, then a couple of the others. And then it was Janet's turn. She looked nervous as she mounted a bright red toboggan. But then, thought Rachel unkindly, she pretty much always looked nervous.

Tammy gave her an encouraging shove and she was off, flying faster and faster down the smooth, glittering snow-path. And then it happened. The main frame of the toboggan seemed to detach itself from the wooden slats beneath. Janet, clinging to the bar in front, zoomed one way on the top half – while the bottom went the other. Screaming, she seemed to be leaping in the snow in a series of wild jerks until she landed heavily and upside-down in a very thick drift.

Everyone came racing down the hill to where her still, inert body lay collapsed in the snow. Rachel pushed her way through them and gently touched Janet's arm. The girl was white with fear and shock, but she allowed Rachel to lift her to a sitting position. Sean crouched beside them both, watching anxiously as Rachel gently checked her over for injuries.

"Thank goodness she's not badly hurt," she said quietly to Sean. "She's obviously very shocked and she's twisted her ankle quite badly. But it could have been a lot worse. I wonder how it happened?"

As Sean carefully helped Janet to her feet, Tammy appeared, carrying the second, lower half of the toboggan which she'd rescued from further down the slope. Her face was grim.

"Screws were loose," she announced. "Or I should say, they were loosened. I've never known a toboggan to come apart like that, not even an old one. And these are fairly new."

Rachel was aghast. Surely – surely not another disaster! "But we checked them. I know we did!" she protested.

Tammy nodded, as puzzled as she was. "I could have sworn we did, too," she agreed. "But maybe there was a structural fault underneath. If that's the case, it should never have been in the cupboard in the first place."

"It wasn't," Rachel said faintly. "Don't you remember? That was one of the red ones that we fetched from the office. I thought those two looked different but I just assumed they were a newer design."

Tammy was still mystified. "Well, we did all the usual checks and they seemed OK," she said. "The only way we could have missed such a big fault is if it was deliberately covered up. But it's hard to see why anyone would do that…"

In an attempt to shake off the awful sense of foreboding that threatened to engulf her, Rachel went and put an arm round Janet. "I am sorry," she said simply. "I really am. I would never, ever have used that toboggan if I'd had any suspicion at all that it was defective."

But Janet just gave her a cold, pained look as she limped along, leaning heavily on Sean's arm. "Yes, well, it's funny how it just happened to be me," she commented. "Either you're very spiteful, Rachel, or you're just plain incompetent."

And as she tossed her head away, Rachel was consumed by a paralysing mixture of rage, guilt and utter, total helplessness.

That evening, the three girls decided to drown their sorrows at Karl's bar, in the village. Lisa, still bruised from her brush with danger on the Santa Claus pass, listened with amazement to Rachel's story of the toboggan disaster.

"This is becoming like the holiday from hell," she said, horrified. "Someone's obviously trying to sabotage us. First all my flags magically changed from black to blue. And now your toboggan... Was it the only one?"

Tammy nodded. "As far as we could tell. We had them all checked over again at the Centre when we got back, and it does look as if the red one had been tampered with. We just checked the screws on the outside. It never occurred to us to look at the bolts holding the whole contraption together."

"Fortunately," commented Rachel, who prided herself on her efficiency and always hated to be in the wrong, "we're not going to be held responsible. But I still feel responsible. And Janet isn't making it any easier."

She gestured over to a far corner of the bar where Janet sat, with a martyred expression, her foot ostentatiously bandaged and propped on a stool. Sean sat next to her, mournfully staring into his beer, and shaking his head at Mike, who was beckoning him over to the pool table.

"Another bottle of wine for my favourite customer," said a deep, teasing voice. Karl had appeared at the bar and was looking intently at Rachel. She found herself smiling back at him. At least someone was pleased to see her.

He leaned over and murmured: "I hope you have not forgotten our little bargain." She blushed, hoping the others couldn't overhear.

"We must make a date, yes?" Karl went on. "How about tomorrow afternoon? You come here – and bring your swimming costume, yes? I have a nice surprise for you."

Rachel nodded, and muttered, "OK," still hoping that the others hadn't noticed. But as soon as Karl had turned away, Tammy rounded on her.

"I thought I'd warned you about him," she said. "Some women just won't be told."

"He's just a friend," Rachel protested. Lisa and Tammy spluttered into their wine glasses.

"Oh, please!" said Lisa. "Can't you think up a better line than that?"

"He's a Taurus, Rachel," Tammy added. "Which is reason enough to steer clear of him. Oh, no – talking of bad signs. Look over there!"

Sadly, she nodded to the door. Jason and Gudrun had just walked in. Hand in hand. They were so engrossed in each other, they didn't even notice the others, as they made their way to a little table right at the other side of the bar.

All day, Jason had been planning his next move. He'd greeted his chalet party with his usual easy courtesy at breakfast time and ushered them out to the slopes as cheerfully as he always did. He'd seen to someone's request for a new pair of boots, handled a traveller's cheque problem and even taken some of his group skating in the afternoon. And, being Jason, he'd also managed to prepare a complicated chicken dish involving a great deal of cream and brandy, plus four different vegetables.

But all that time, at the back of his mind, he'd been formulating his strategy. It was while he was peeling the carrots and paring them into tiny matchstick shapes that he thought hardest about what he was going to do.

For several days, ever since he and Gudrun had made those afternoon pastries together, Jason had been in seventh heaven. He worshipped her as much as ever – more, really, he reflected, now that he'd started to get to know her. She seemed happy to spend time with him, and happiest of all when they were cooking together, or swapping recipes. Even though she was a far better skier than he was, she'd condescended to go on the slopes with him on free afternoons – she even seemed to enjoy it. But now, Jason told himself, chopping the carrots fiercely, now it was time to make a proper move. Tonight, he resolved, was the night. They'd already agreed to meet after supper and walk into town together for a drink. It was the perfect opportunity to let her know how he felt. He just had to find the right moment.

But it wasn't as easy as all that. They walked side by side along the little path to the village, quite crowded at this time of the evening as holiday-makers explored the bars and nearby taverns. Soon, as usual, they were talking animatedly about cooking and food, and Gudrun began to warm up a little, as she always did after a little while when they were together.

It took all his courage to reach out and take her hand. And then, when she didn't object, he was so delirious with triumph that he could barely concentrate on what she was saying, even when they were sitting in a secluded corner of Karl's busy tavern, chatting happily. Gudrun was telling him stories about her childhood in Germany – how she loved the countryside but had always yearned to travel. "So that is why I took care to learn everything that I would need," she explained. "I learned to cook, to speak languages, to do business, everything. I wish to go to many places, meet many people."

"I wish you'd come to England then," Jason said earnestly. Gudrun's face remained impassive, but she said nothing. "I – I would love it if you'd visit," Jason added. She smiled fleetingly and seemed suddenly sad. She got up and Jason followed her outside.

On the way back to the Dream Ticket chalets, she was silent. Jason was beginning to feel desperate. Impetuously, he grabbed her by the arm and drew her away from the path to a nearby bench facing the skating lake.

For a few moments they sat side by side, watching the reflection of the moon in the shimmering ice. It was very beautiful. "It's no good," whispered Jason softly. "I'm going to have to kiss you."

Very gently, his heart pounding, he leaned

towards her and drew her face to his. At last, trembling, he pressed his lips to hers. Her mouth felt firm, almost cool, but she didn't resist. Jason, joyfully pulling her closer and kissing her again, was aware only of his need for her, of wanting to hold her and crush her in his arms. Yet, somehow, she remained as unreachable and remote as ever. And even more desirable.

9

A piercing scream rent the air. There was a startled silence in the Red Chalet dining room. Then another scream, followed by a series of thumps and clatters.

Rachel glanced anxiously round the room. There was Heidi, who'd arrived early for once and was busily buttering toast and handing round scones. Brett, looking tired, was fondling Nina's hand as she toyed with a sliver of melon. Janet, predictably, had been pouring a cup of tea which she now promptly spilt all over the floor. Sean looked pained. Laura glanced to the ceiling in mock despair before resignedly helping to mop up the mess.

Tommy, who was tucking in to a huge plate of eggs and bacon, paused briefly to comment, still chewing: "That'll be my lady luck, I expect, pulling the first wobbly of the day. Nothing to worry about, I shouldn't think."

He was right, Rachel realized. Jonquil was the

only member of the group who was missing. Everyone else was tucking into breakfast. But Tommy wasn't so right about there being nothing to worry about.

Jonquil now appeared in the doorway looking pale and tragic. "My jewellery!" she announced dramatically. "My beautiful works. Gone – all gone!"

Tommy still couldn't quite bring himself to stop eating. He shovelled another forkful into his mouth before commenting: "Now calm down, angel. What are you talking about? What's gone?"

"My jewellery," repeated Jonquil. "You imbecile. Surely you know what I mean by my jewellery. It's what keeps us alive and in business, remember."

Unperturbed, Tommy said patiently: "Yes, darlin', of course I know. The jewellery is in the safe as usual, in our room. I had it with me yesterday on a couple of visits and then locked it all away when I got back. So I don't know what you're on about. Drama queen," he added in a muffled whisper to Nina, who didn't respond.

"Not that jewellery, nincompoop!" snapped Jonquil. "I'm talking about the special collection. The musical sequence and the opals. The ones we were planning to show to Serge Anton, remember? The day after Christmas? Well, what am I going to show him now?"

And suddenly she crumpled and tears began to splash down her face. Rachel darted over to her and led her gently to a chair. "Are you sure you haven't just mislaid them?" she asked gently.

Jonquil rallied for a moment, her eyes darkening.

"No – no! This is theft. Someone has taken my most perfect pieces. Someone who knows where I keep them, and someone who knows how much they mean to me." She turned balefully to Nina, who was cutting a tiny piece of melon and concentrating hard on transferring it to her mouth.

"Oh, for heaven's sake, Jonquil!" protested Brett, horrified. But Nina just shrugged. "Don't look at me," she said, with a magnificent air of boredom. "I'm not the least bit interested in you or your so-called designs. They're just not my style, really. Sorry."

Jonquil looked furious. Tommy was just beginning to be concerned. Everyone else was rather subdued. By now Marjorie had appeared, without warning, as she often seemed to do at any sign of trouble. "Well, first of all we'd better establish where you think the jewellery was and who might have had access to it, dear," she said.

"I definitely had it yesterday," Jonquil said. "I was showing it to you, Rachel, remember? Then I left it in a special place all day while I was out. This morning I went to look for it and it was gone."

"So who was around yesterday who might have seen the intruder?" asked Marjorie tactfully. It was obvious she really meant: Who had an opportunity to steal the goods? "Heidi, did you see anyone suspicious when you were here yesterday?"

"Oh, but I did not come yesterday," Heidi said. "I got the message I was not needed. So I stay at home."

"And who did the house instead?" asked Marjorie. There was an awful silence. Rachel felt a sudden chill as all those pairs of eyes turned to gaze at her.

"You did, didn't you?" accused Jonquil nastily. "And you saw my musical pieces. And you saw me put them under the pillow. And then you were alone here, going through the bedrooms!"

The next three hours passed slowly and painfully like a nightmare. The police were called, the chalet searched. Rachel and Lisa's apartment was searched, and Rachel's room turned upside-down. Rachel was taken to the police station for questioning – and she herself was searched, which was probably the most humiliating part of the whole thing. Nothing was found and even Marjorie, eventually, had to admit that it didn't really seem all that likely that Rachel was the thief, especially as nothing had been found and there was really no evidence of her guilt.

"But you must admit, things have been going awry for you lately, my dear," Marjorie said, much later, over what she called a "cosy little chat".

Rachel was silent. She hadn't realized that Marjorie was aware of her catalogue of mishaps. "Oh, it's my job to notice these things," Marjorie was saying, as if reading her mind. "Ill-fitting boots ... the faulty toboggan ... now this. It's just not like you, Rachel. You come with such a good record. Management material, that's what I was told. But good managers do not allow things to go wrong, Rachel. Good managers know that the customer is always right and never, ever speak disrespectfully to them."

Rachel blushed, remembering her outburst to Brett on that first day. She hadn't realized then that he'd reported her behaviour. Just my luck, she thought gloomily.

"Good managers," Marjorie continued, "see that everything runs like clockwork. Detail, my dear, that's what matters."

"But I do pay attention to detail," protested Rachel, stung at the attack on what she considered her best qualities. "I love organizing things properly. But this time – well, it's as if someone's got it in for me. I just can't believe it's a coincidence that all these awful things are happening, and every single one has been made to look as if it's my fault."

"Now, Rachel, that's no way to deal with this," warned Marjorie. "If you've made mistakes you must vow to do better. There's no point looking for someone to blame."

Rachel sighed, and images flashed into her mind of Janet – Janet accusing her of stealing her husband; then the burned cake; then Jason's missing key-ring; then the toboggan accident. She gasped as she remembered how Janet had been helped back to the chalet, then left there alone while the others had returned to the Northern Heights complex. Janet had had the perfect opportunity to take Jonquil's jewels – while making it look as though Rachel had done it.

But how could she even suggest such a thing to Marjorie? Even now, Marjorie was saying kindly,

"I know perfectly well you didn't do it, dear. It would be so foolish, for a rep to steal from a client."

"Oh, thanks a lot!" Rachel retorted. "I suppose you think I would have done it, then, if I could have been sure of not being caught. Well, what about honesty? What about trust? I'm not a thief, Marjorie, whatever the circumstances."

"Of course not, dear," answered Marjorie. "That's what I was saying, but you must stop these unfortunate things from happening, Rachel. Just be more careful from now on."

"Well, how, exactly, was this one my fault?" Rachel asked, exasperated.

"Oh, you know," Marjorie said vaguely. "Security, vigilance, mind on the job. Remember, Rachel, you're a Dream Ticket person and that means you must put your clients' needs first, twenty four hours a day. So that's settled then. No more mistakes, no more misery. So glad we've had this little chat. Best to get these things out in the open, I always say."

As she made her way back to the apartment, Rachel was grinding her teeth in frustration. Marjorie always came up with phrases that you might read on a greetings card, or embroidered on a cushion. "No more mistakes, no more misery," Rachel repeated to herself. It was OK as a slogan, but it certainly wasn't any help with the problems that seemed to be closing in on her.

As soon as she got back to her room she rang Jack. He was sympathetic, but somehow sounded very far away. "Well, of course no one seriously could have thought you were a thief," he said, as if it was all a bit of a joke. "When you found a pound coin on the street you insisted on handing it in to the police. Remember that time you went running after the woman who'd dropped a silk scarf – and it turned out she'd been throwing it away! I mean, you're so honest that you don't understand the rules of Happy Families – let alone Poker!" Rachel knew he was just trying to cheer her up, but that wasn't what she needed. "I wish you could be here," she whispered, feeling very lonely suddenly.

"I know sweetheart, I know," Jack answered. "But let's just imagine. I'm looking at the phone now and pretending it's you. You look at yours and imagine it's me. And when I count to three let's do a great big noisy kiss, OK? One, two, mmm..."

"Aha, one beautiful English girl – all for me," said Karl as Rachel poked her head round the door of the pâtisserie. It was later that afternoon. Amid all the panic and confusion of the morning she'd completely forgotten about their date. It was Lisa, desperately sorry for her friend and casting around for anything that might cheer her up, who'd remembered.

"Go on, Rache – you might as well," she'd urged her. "He seems kind of fun. And anyway, you did promise..."

So here she was, being led gently round the back of the pâtisserie, through the kitchen past delicious-looking rows of sticky cakes, and hot, sweet-smelling ovens, and out of the back door to a little courtyard. "Here is covered in flowers in spring," Karl told her. "You should see it. I hope very much to show you one day. Now, follow, please – I have a surprise…"

On the opposite side of the courtyard was Karl's house, really just a bungalow with a wooden platform leading from the french windows out into a secluded garden. A green cover was thrown over a raised circular shape in the middle of the wooden deck. Karl strode over to it and ripped the cloth away with a flourish.

"This is my surprise," he announced proudly. Rachel stared in amazement at what looked like a steaming, swirling paddling pool. "Come," he ordered. "First we get changed."

He showed her into the bathroom and very discreetly disappeared somewhere else to get changed. A few minutes later they were standing in his living room, Rachel in her most sensible, unrevealing costume, Karl in the tightest pair of trunks she had ever seen, looking out of the french windows on to glistening snow and droplets of ice hanging from the trees like transparent earrings.

Karl took her hand. "Come, I show you," he said gently. "Do not worry about the cold. I promise you will like…"

One moment the frozen air was whipping round her body, pinching her with exquisite cruelty. And then she was being cradled by the steaming hot water in the tub which swirled round her, caressing her legs, her arms, her whole body right up to her neck. She sat on a ledge inside the Jacuzzi, allowing the floaty, pampering heat to envelop her.

Karl sat watching her for a while, smiling lazily as he stretched into the water, leaning back into the foamy waves. "It is good, no?" he said after a while. "I have watched you, Rachel. You work so hard, you take everything so seriously. You need to relax. I want you to be happy, to let go a little..." It was almost like being hypnotized, Rachel thought, as she leaned back and allowed her mind to drift.

"This is the first time I've relaxed for days and days," she said almost to herself. "Everything's been so horrible." And she found herself pouring out her troubles, telling Karl about the series of disasters, all so unlike her but all, somehow, connected, as if someone was deliberately trying to sabotage her.

Karl let her talk. He lay in the hot tub, eyes half closed, listening and occasionally grunting. "Now I am beginning to understand," he said at last. "You are not like the girl I met last week on the slopes. Then I wanted to know you more because you were so bright, so confident. I thought yes, this girl, she is fun. But then each time I see you there is more tension, more frowning."

He edged towards her and reached behind her neck. With slow, sure fingers he began to massage her shoulders. "I can feel the knots," he murmured. "Here, and here – Rachel, these knots are your unhappiness. We must get rid of them."

It felt wonderful – so wonderful that Rachel

allowed herself to sink into the sensations of warmth and tenderness. "You must not worry, Rachel," Karl murmured as his hands massaged her neck. "I think maybe you are making too much of these incidents. But if someone is making trouble for you, then we will stop them, yes?"

Rachel could have wept, there and then. Karl was actually making her feel better. He'd managed to calm her fears but to take them seriously all at the same time. She felt she could stay here for ever, basking in the magic of the hot tub, the sharp cold outside, the magic of Karl's fingers...

But after a while he took her hand and helped her out of the tub. For just a few seconds the freezing air gripped her again, but it wasn't long before she was curled up in an armchair in front of a wood fire, wrapped in a huge fluffy towel. Karl appeared a few minutes later with two steaming mugs of hot chocolate. He was fully dressed.

He crossed the polished floorboards of the living room and placed the mugs on the large glass coffee table before settling down on a rug by the fire at Rachel's feet. She took a sip of the chocolate. It was delicious. But she had to put the mug back quickly because her hand was trembling. She was aware of Karl, watching her intently from where he was leaning on the floor. Their eyes locked.

Then he knelt and leaned up to her until their lips met. Rachel closed her eyes, melting into that first gentle kiss, wanting it to go on for ever. Karl cradled her in his arms, pulling her closer and closer towards him until she slid down on to the floor. With a skilled, unhurried movement he lowered her down beside him until they were both stretched out in front of the fire, its flames leaping over them.

Karl's expert hands were moving right down her back now and his kisses were becoming more insistent as he began to pull the towel away from her shoulders. Underneath, she was wearing nothing. But as his fingers came into contact with her bare flesh she suddenly jerked away from him, horrified. It was as though a spell had been broken and she was back in the real world again.

"Sorry, Karl – I hadn't realized how late it was," she blustered. "I've got to go."

Minutes later, she was flying fully dressed out of the front door – in such a rush that she didn't even hear Karl calling after her, "So – when am I going to see you again?"

10

"So what were you doing with him this afternoon?" Lisa demanded later that evening. The two girls had decided to have an early night and decorate their tiny Christmas tree. "Come on, Rachel – I am your best friend, remember? You can tell me."

"Oh, nothing much," Rachel replied airily.

"But Rachel – what about Jack?" asked Lisa, her eyes wide with shock.

"Oh, that's rich, coming from you!" Rachel retorted. "Look at the way you've been carrying on with Jean-Pierre. And Alex is actually going to be here the day after tomorrow. Then what are you going to do?"

Lisa shrugged. "Well, that's different. Jean-Pierre knows all about Alex, and he's got a girlfriend, too. So it's not a problem, is it? No one's going to get hurt."

Involuntarily, she blushed as she remembered her last encounter with Jean-Pierre, the urgency of their embraces and the rush of passion she had felt for him.

"Don't kid yourself, Lisa," Rachel advised. "You're playing with fire, and I suppose I am as well. Only – well, I didn't mean it to be like this."

"Nor did I," agreed Lisa.

"It's not as if anything has happened – not really," Rachel added.

"Nor with me," Lisa put in eagerly. "Nothing's actually happened."

"But it could have," Rachel mused.

"And it still might," added Lisa.

They stared at each other, confused but defiant.

"I love Jack, but it's not as if he owned me," said Rachel defensively. "I mean, there's nothing wrong with a bit of a holiday romance, is there?"

"Nothing at all. I mean, they might be doing exactly the same thing," said Lisa. She started to hook chocolate reindeer and snowmen on to the little tree with studied concentration.

Rachel, who'd just had a shower, began to rub her hair vigorously with a towel. "Would you mind?" she asked suddenly. "If Alex had been seeing someone?"

Lisa thought for a moment, then grabbed a handful of tinsel and showered it over the tree. "I'd kill him," she admitted. "How about you?"

"Me, too," agreed Rachel. "Do you think we should be feeling guilty?"

"No," said Lisa at once, still busy with the tree. There was a pause. Then they both said in unison: "Yes!" and began to laugh hysterically.

"You know, I think Karl just happened to come

along at the right time," said Rachel thoughtfully. "I was feeling so rotten – and he listened, and took me seriously." She started telling Lisa how miserable she had been, and how convinced she was now that someone was trying to sabotage her.

"And at least he understood," she explained. "He didn't try and tell me I was paranoid and making it all up."

"Rachel, look – I'm sorry, OK," Lisa said, genuinely concerned for her friend. "I admit it, I thought you were jumping to conclusions before. But it's different now. I think you must be right. There have been just too many coincidences. And I reckon it's time we did something about it."

Rachel eyed her doubtfully, hardly able to believe what she was hearing. "Really? You're sure?" Lisa nodded.

Relief flooded through Rachel as she realized that at last she had a real ally – someone who was on her side and believed in her. "So – so what can we do?"

Lisa carefully attached a silver star and a golden moon to the tree, thinking hard. "Well, suppose it is Janet who's been doing all these things – to get at you," she mused. "She's bound to do something else fairly soon, isn't she? I think we should just try and watch her, get one step ahead and see if we can catch her in the act."

Rachel brightened at the idea of a plan of action. "Do you mean, we have to follow her?"

"If we can," agreed Lisa. "Let's start tomorrow – between us, we'll have her covered all day. It'll be harder the next day because that's when Alex is arriving. In time for the Christmas Eve party."

"Lucky thing!" sighed Rachel automatically. "I wish Jack was coming." For a moment, she remembered the events of the afternoon – those moments on the floor in front of the fire, Karl crushing her in his arms, their lips melded together. But, strangely, she felt detached from the scene – almost as though it had nothing to do with her. "I really wish he was here now…"

It was lunchtime the following day and Northern Heights was suddenly teeming with hungry, jostling crowds, stamping the snow off their boots and crowding into the bar. A sudden fierce snowstorm had driven everyone off the slopes and down to the village.

Lisa, Rachel and Tammy sat together round an enormous, steaming bowl of fondue. "I just can't get the hang of it," Lisa was saying, winding the melted cheese round and round her iron tong. "How do you actually get any of it into your mouth? It's like trying to eat chewing gum."

Tammy laughed. "Here, let me show you! First you're supposed to get a cube of this bread on the fork and then you dip it – like this…"

Rachel glanced round the crowded room with her usual quick stock-taking. There was Jonquil, looking tragic and sipping an elegant glass of Kir. Tommy was beside her, trying not to show how much he was enjoying his three-layered hamburger. Brett was absent-mindedly fondling Nina's hand while she nonchalantly tucked into a toasted sandwich.

Two fresh, rosy faces appeared in the doorway – Jason and Gudrun had just arrived. Rachel felt Tammy stiffen beside her. "You know, I did my chart again last night," Tammy said, making a brave attempt to sound cheerful. "Apparently, there's going to be a massive upheaval when Aquarius moves into its solar descent. Do you suppose that means the snowstorm? Because then maybe he'll need to switch to a more empathetic sign..."

Rachel squeezed her arm. "Don't waste your time, Tammy. If you must do those charts why not use them to find someone else? A nice, strapping Scorpio for example, or a sensitive Sagittarius."

But all the time she was speaking, Rachel was watching another group, across the room. Mike, as usual, was trying to persuade Sean to join him for a game of snooker. Then Laura piped up: "Well if you're not keen, why don't we try table tennis? I mean, we're obviously stuck here for a while so we may as well have some fun."

"That's an idea!" said Sean, eagerly draining his glass of beer. "I love ping pong – we used to play at home all the time. We had a table in the garage."

"Get you!" teased Laura. "I had to learn the hard way – at Girl Guides. I think I've got a badge for it somewhere."

"Did I ever mention that I used to be ping pong champion for the South West?" put in Mike.

"South West what?" retorted Sean. "South West corner of the playground?"

They were so caught up with their laughing, teasing banter that they didn't notice that Janet had stopped eating her plate of spaghetti and was staring at them, her face white and blank and angry. Only Rachel, observing them from across the room, saw the fury in her eyes. And only Rachel heard the whispered exchange.

"Great!" snarled Janet. "How am I supposed to play table tennis with my foot?"

"You can watch," muttered Sean.

"No thanks!" she retorted. "You three can play on your own."

With that the trio noisily made their way to the games room, but Janet did not follow them. Only Rachel saw her quietly, unobtrusively slip away.

"Quick!" Rachel hissed to the others. "It's happening! She's going off alone."

"Thank goodness for that," said Lisa. "Now I don't have to have any more cheesy mess."

They quickly made their way out of the bar, a bemused Tammy trailing after them. Rachel insisted that they trail Janet properly, without letting her realize they were following her. This meant a lot of ducking behind walls and trees as they progressed along the little lane in the falling snow.

Lisa kept getting the giggles. "I feel like Nancy Drew," she said. "Don't you think what we're doing might strike some people as a little strange?"

"It was your idea, remember!" Rachel said in a loud whisper.

"Will someone please tell me what's going on!" cried Tammy plaintively. Both girls turned on her with a giant "Sshh!", then proceeded to fill her in on their plan to catch Janet in some telling act of betrayal.

They didn't have to shadow her for very long. Predictably enough, she simply made her way back to Red Chalet, still limping from her toboggan accident.

They waited for five, then ten minutes. "I'm getting cold," Lisa complained. "Why can't we just go and confront her? Whatever it is she's doing she'll have done it by now."

"No, we have to give her a bit of time to settle down and make sure she's alone," said Rachel firmly.

At last, after twenty frozen minutes, Rachel judged it safe to lead the others very quietly through the front door. They stood in the dining room, listening carefully. Where was she? And what was she doing?

Suddenly, Rachel grabbed the others. She'd heard something. From upstairs, came the sound of the tearing of paper, followed by a sob. Then another tearing sound. What on earth was Janet up to?

Stealthily, Rachel led the way up the stairs. The three girls stood uncertainly on the landing, listening. Sure enough, there was more tearing, a clunking sound, more sobbing. The noise was coming from Janet and Sean's bedroom.

Rachel tiptoed along the corridor, stopped outside the room with her hand on the doorknob for a few moments and then, decisively, flung open the door. There, on the bed, was Janet, a pad of paper and a pen in her hand, her face creased with tears.

"Rachel!" she gulped. "What are you doing here? This is my room, you know."

"Well, I heard some funny sounds," Rachel began. "I wondered if you were OK." Vaguely, she was aware that things were not quite right in the room. The floor was littered with crumpled pieces of paper. A waste paper bin had been overturned. A suitcase was open on the bed, piled with clothes which spilled over on to the floor.

"No, I'm not OK, thank you very much," said Janet shakily. "And why don't you mind your own business for once?"

"Well, maybe it is her business," chimed in Lisa loyally.

"What do you mean?" snivelled Janet, not looking as if she much cared.

"Oh, come off it, Janet, you must know what I mean," Lisa went on, ignoring Rachel's frantic signals to shut up. "It's obvious you hate Rachel for some reason, and you've gone out of your way to persecute her. So what little nasty trick are you dreaming up this time, eh?"

Janet looked puzzled. "What – what tricks?"

Lisa's arm swept round the room, taking in the general air of chaos. "Well, you've already tried to make it look as if Rachel stole Jonquil's jewellery," she said. "That didn't work. So now, obviously, you're ransacking your own room so you can blame Rachel for that, as well. But how you're going to make it look like her fault is beyond me. What did you have in mind? Footprints? Finger-prints? Traces of DNA?"

Ignoring Janet's gape of amazement, Lisa stormed over to her and snatched the pad from her trembling hand. "Oh, right – this'll be the incriminating evidence, I expect." But as she began to read what Janet had written, it was Lisa's turn to look puzzled.

"But – but what's this?" she began.

"Quite," commented Janet, mustering some dignity despite the fact that her eyes were red and swollen and she was still crying. "Like I said, it's none of your business. But as you can see, you're on the wrong trail, completely."

Rachel looked over one shoulder, Tammy the other, as Lisa held the scrawled piece of paper. "Dear Sean," it read. "I've tried every way I can but it's clear that I can't make you happy. I love you as much as ever but being with you is just too painful. Don't try and get in touch. It's over. Janet."

The three girls stared, horrified, at the unhappy woman sprawled on the bed. "Hope you like it," she said brokenly. "It still needs polishing, but as you can see, I'd already done ten other versions." Their eyes travelled to the crumpled, discarded notes all over the floor and to the waste paper bin, which had clearly been kicked over in distress.

"Janet – you're not seriously going to leave Sean, are you?" Rachel asked after a long, painful silence.

"What do you think?" snarled Janet scornfully.

"But – but he loves you," Rachel said. Janet snorted.

"No, really," Rachel persisted. "I know he does. You see – when you saw us together that first time, in the bar, he was just telling me how much he loves you and – and saying it was hard to get through to you at the moment. He really, really does love you. But you don't seem to want to hear it."

"No, instead you rushed to the conclusion that Rachel was trying to steal him away from you. And strangely enough, that's when all these nasty things started to happen." Lisa had a feeling things weren't quite going to plan, but she wasn't prepared to give up too easily.

Janet sighed. "I've told you, I haven't had anything to do with playing tricks on Rachel, or anyone else. I don't even know what you mean. All I've been thinking about is Sean. Sean and me – and all the things that get in the way of our happiness. Like you," she said to Rachel. "It's true, I did think you fancied him. And that was just another awful obstacle between us. But I never tried to get back at you, Rachel. I wouldn't do that. You're not worth it."

Rachel took a deep breath and tried again. "I can't make you like me, Janet. In fact, I don't much care if you loathe me. But what I said about Sean is true. He's madly in love with you."

"Oh yeah?" said Janet in disbelief. "If that's so, why does he spend so much time ignoring me, or putting me down, or letting his friends put me down, always making out how much better they are than me…"

"Well, maybe you don't make it very easy for him," Tammy chimed in unexpectedly. "You can be a miserable old cow you know, Janet. Men don't like endless whingeing. What sign is Sean, anyway? I bet he's a Taurus. He looks like one. You see!" She beamed round at everyone as Janet grudgingly nodded. "Well, that explains a lot. Taurus guys can't take drippy women. I bet you weren't drippy when he fell in love with you, but you are now. You're a right pain to be with."

"Steady on!" Rachel intervened, alarmed at Tammy's harshness. "That's not fair – and it's not true, either."

"Yes it is," Janet said sadly. "It hurts to hear it, but I think Tammy's right, and I'm grateful to you for being so honest. So what do you think I should do?"

"I'd forget about all this pathetic drama, love, if I were you. It'll only drive him away. Just be yourself and make him love you again. It'll work if you want it to."

A little while later the four girls gathered in the kitchen for a cup of tea. Somehow, Janet had been persuaded to unpack her things, throw away all her goodbye notes, and try again. Tammy's words had made sense to her but so, also, had Rachel's, once she'd made up her mind to listen.

Between the four of them there was a strange new camaraderie – almost a friendship.

"I propose a toast," Janet suddenly announced solemnly. They looked at her expectantly as she raised her teacup. "I now take it you all believe it's not me who's been cooking up all these accidents for Rachel." They all nodded, even Lisa. "And given that it was me who fell off the toboggan, and me who got the wrong boots, I'm not exactly mad about this crazy person myself."

"How do you mean, the wrong boots?" frowned Rachel. "I thought all the coincidences started after that."

"Only because you thought it was me making them happen," Janet pointed out. "And the boots happened before I had a motive. Right? Before I saw you with Sean."

Rachel nodded again, staring at Janet with renewed concentration.

"So, since it wasn't me, that could have been the first act of sabotage," Janet went on. "Maybe whoever is doing it just got lucky when I started hating you. Which brings me to my toast. To the four of us – between us, we're going to catch the real villain."

"I'll drink to that," said Rachel fervently. And the four of them clinked their mugs together in a solemn, heartfelt promise.

11

The next morning was Christmas Eve. Lisa was sitting nervously in the Alpine Bar, knocking back glass after glass of sparkling apple juice, her usually cheerful face creased with tension. Alex was due to arrive any moment.

"Anyone would think you weren't looking forward to seeing him," commented Rachel drily.

"Of course I am!" snapped Lisa. Then, after a pause, she added: "Well, most of me is. It's just – you know … I don't know if things are going to be the same."

"Surely you're not referring to Jean-Pierre?" Rachel probed, half shocked, half teasing. "I thought he had a girlfriend? I thought you two were supposed to be a quick fling?"

"Yes, well, absolutely, that's all it is … er, was," Lisa corrected herself. "He has nothing to do with my feelings for Alex at all. I'm just on edge, that's all. Which is hardly surprising since he's already over an hour late and you know how I hate that. I get all knotted up between being furious at him for not being there on time and frantic with worrying that he's been in some terrible accident."

Rachel laughed. "Well, you should have got used to it by now. I don't think Alex has ever managed to be on time for anything in his life. He was born that way."

But as she spoke a familiar figure appeared in the doorway – tall, gangling, untidy, an old-fashioned rucksack slung over his shabby green anorak, his unruly mop of blond hair escaping from a knitted navy blue hat.

"Alex!" shrieked Lisa, leaping up and rushing towards him. "Oh, Alex darling!" And then she flung herself into his arms, hugging him tight. It felt wonderful to be with him again, to feel his familiar warmth, see his sweet, lopsided smile.

After a minute or so she pulled away from him and looked him up and down. She frowned. "Have you been looking after yourself?" she demanded. "You're looking awfully thin and sort of ... bedraggled."

Alex grinned. "I love it when you fuss over me," he said. "Other women may shower their lovers with red roses and chocolates, or dress up in slinky black numbers with high, high heels. But mine shows me she loves me by checking up on my fibre intake and counting my calories. I'm surprised you haven't asked me when I last went to the toilet."

"Well, I can't help it," said Lisa, falling into their familiar banter. "I have to treat you a little bit like a child sometimes because you behave like one.

Are you still into those magnum bottles of Coke you used to be so addicted to?"

"It's a secret," said Alex. "Anyhow, aren't you going to invite me to sit down and tell you why I look, as you so lovingly put it, bedraggled?"

"Over here," called Rachel from across the bar. "We've saved a seat for you." She kissed Alex affectionately on both cheeks as he shambled over to the table. "Oh, it's good to see you," she added warmly. "Now drink this hot chocolate before you do anything else. I feel an Alex story coming on."

"Oh, it's nothing really," Alex said when he'd warmed up a little, and drained his cup of chocolate. "The flight was fine, and I got my train connection and everything." He beamed at the girls, obviously expecting them to look impressed. "But there was this – this avalanche."

"What!" they shrieked in unison.

"Well, OK – not quite an avalanche," he conceded. "But all this snow tumbled down from this steep cutaway on one side of the train. And it blocked the track. And we were miles from anywhere. So they asked for volunteers – and the passengers had to get out and dig the snow away. It took hours – and I was frozen stiff. Especially as I'd only just arrived. Imagine, only a few hours ago I was wearing shorts and baring my chest on the beach. Of course, I was told to stop because it made all the girls so uncontrollably excited."

Lisa laughed at him fondly. It was going to be fine, she told herself, relieved. Alex was the same old Alex, and she loved him just as much as ever.

After she'd taken him to her room in the apartment to unpack, she insisted that they go to the slopes.

"I haven't been skiing since I was at school," protested Alex.

"All the more reason to get started," Lisa said firmly. "Besides, it's like cycling. Once you've got the hang of it you never forget."

At first, she was rather impressed with Alex. She had expected him to be clumsy and a bit ungainly, because Alex was not exactly an outdoor type. It was always Lisa who was mad about exercise and fitness, always keen to try new sports. Alex usually preferred more sedentary pursuits. Like sitting around not doing much.

So Lisa was pleased to see him plunging down the lower nursery slopes – even if it was with more enthusiasm than skill. They were happily zigzagging down another, slightly steeper slope when they were overtaken by what felt like an express train streaking past them.

Lisa caught her breath. It was Jean-Pierre. He was undoubtedly showing off, sweeping effortlessly down a steep incline at what seemed like eighty miles an hour, his jet black ski suit shimmering against the white snow. As he came to a halt and waved to them, Lisa couldn't help comparing his handsome, well-toned physique, his sleek style and chiselled good looks with Alex, slightly round-shouldered, legs bent, his pale face pink with sun and wind. Somehow, his good-humoured grin seemed so goofy compared with Jean-Pierre's gleaming smile; his thin chest looked almost hollow next to Jean-Pierre's rippling muscles. And oh, that anorak...

"Alex, I'd like you to meet Jean-Pierre, a friend of mine. He's a ski instructor," Lisa explained, hoping she wasn't blushing too obviously. The two men eyed each other as they shook hands.

Then Jean-Pierre smiled his most charming smile and said, "I have heard much about you, Alex. I hope you will enjoy your stay here. You are ... some lucky guy." And with that, he zipped off down the slope, leaving a shimmer of powdered snow in his wake.

"Nice bloke," commented Alex amiably. But for Lisa, the sun had gone in just a little. And for the rest of the day a cloud hung over her – a cloud of doubt and unrest.

Jason hovered over the simmering saucepan, waiting for his magic sauce to thicken. Tonight, he was convinced, would be the night for him and Gudrun. Not only had she agreed to go to the Christmas Eve party with him. She'd even said that she would have dinner with him first. He'd already prepared one meal for his chalet – to be served by his helper. Gudrun was doing the same. So now he was concentrating on a special recipe which he just knew would make Gudrun fall madly in love with him. Or at least, that was the plan.

Happily, he hummed to himself as he tasted the mixture, then added pepper; tasted again, sprinkled on a little nutmeg and a scattering of chilli powder. He had an apartment to himself, as he was the only guy. He'd lit a fire in the living room although the apartment was already very warm. He'd set the table romantically for two, with pretty red napkins on a white cloth and long-stemmed wine glasses; red candles stood ready in star-shaped holders, and he'd even managed to decorate a log with berries and gold-painted leaves and pine cones.

He uncorked a bottle of wine and poured a little into a glass. With steady concentration he added a few drops to his sauce, then tasted it again. Satisfied, he finished off the rest of the glass, then poured the sauce carefully over a dish of chicken breasts and put the dish in the oven, next to the little cheese and spinach parcels he'd wrapped himself.

There was a rap on the door. Jason felt a rush of excitement when he saw Gudrun. As usual, she looked ravishing in a slinky black dress and her usual jet black earrings. Everything about her shimmered, thought Jason, admiring her glossy blonde hair, creamy skin and glittering blue eyes. She sniffed appreciatively as she slid past him into the living room.

"Mmm, that smell is so good," she said. "Jason, I think you are a genius in the kitchen."

Jason beamed. "Well, I hope you're going to like what I've cooked up for you," he answered, thinking about some of the plans he'd cooked up that Gudrun didn't know about yet.

Soon they were sitting opposite each other at the table, tucking into Jason's wafer thin pastry hors-d'oeuvres. Gudrun was obviously impressed

– so impressed that she said very little, just concentrated on the delicious vegetable parcels, swimming in a pale green leek sauce.

She was still very quiet over the main course, until Jason poured out the wine and they clinked their glasses together. At that moment, their eyes met. Jason felt his knees go weak as he gazed at her. It had to be now, he decided. Somehow, he'd have to begin to tell her a little of what he felt for her – how much he wanted her. He summoned all his courage, drew in his breath, and was about to speak.

But, to his surprise, Gudrun got in first.

"Jason," she said earnestly, her penetrating eyes still boring into his. "Dear Jason, there's something I want to say. You see, I have become very fond of you and also, something that is not so usual for me, I trust you. And that is why I know I can ask you this, even though it is – difficult..."

Downstairs in Rachel and Lisa's apartment there was tension in the air. It wasn't as though Lisa and Alex were quarrelling exactly. But Rachel could tell that something was not quite right. She could tell from the way Lisa frowned when Alex appeared in the living room, proudly sporting a denim shirt.

"Are you wearing that for the party?" Lisa asked, an edge in her voice.

"Yeah, I just bought it. What's wrong?"

"Oh, nothing," Lisa assured him hastily. "No, it's – it's really nice." Inwardly, she was cursing herself for being so mean. Alex did look nice in the shirt, in an Alex sort of way. But she couldn't quite banish the picture of Jean-Pierre that flashed into her mind – Jean-Pierre in his shiny ski suit, or his thick black sweater that emphasized those broad, muscular shoulders...

"Well, you look gorgeous," Alex said, reaching out to put his hands on her waist. Lisa was wearing skin-tight satin trousers and a skimpy top that showed her midriff, so his fingers touched her bare skin.

Rachel noticed that she froze just a little, and caught sight of Alex's hurt look. And that was when Rachel made up her mind that the two of them needed cheering up. She'd bought them each a bundle of tiny presents – things like a penknife for Alex and a miniature set of poker dice; Lisa had a tiny set of glass animals, a fridge magnet, ski socks that sang carols.

All she needed to do, she thought, was to slip out of the party, come back to the apartment and put their presents into stockings for them. Then she'd sneak into Lisa's room and leave the stockings there as a surprise. Even if they noticed them that night when they went to bed, it would still be fun – something to bring them closer together.

The Northern Heights party was in full swing when they arrived. Everyone seemed to be dancing. Rachel noticed Brett and Nina, cheek to cheek as usual. Janet seemed very cheerful. Even her foot seemed to have made a miraculous recovery. Dressed all in red, she was dancing wildly with Sean, and winked at Rachel when she saw her. Even Jonquil and Tommy had taken to the dance floor. Marjorie was looking happy for once, daringly bedecked in a sequinned frock, and throwing her head back as Jean-Pierre twirled her round in a kind of mad tango.

Lisa's heart thumped a little too hard when she saw Jean-Pierre, but she decided to ignore it. She was with Alex, wasn't she? Determinedly, she led him by the hand on to the dance floor, then turned and wrapped her arms round his neck.

"Oh, goodness, I'm not sure if I know this one," Alex quipped nervously. She smiled seductively and squeezed harder.

"Don't worry – I'll teach you," she murmured. And, as they began to sway to the music, she told herself that here, truly, was where she belonged.

Meanwhile, Rachel quietly slipped out of the Centre and made her way back to the apartment. It was quite late by now, nearly eleven o'clock. She needed to be back at the party well before midnight, so she had to work quite fast. First she found a pair of red ski socks. She decorated them with some hastily glued-on glitter and some cotton wool for snow. She cut out the words Merry Christmas from a sheet of wrapping paper and stapled them to each sock. Then she stuffed the socks with all the little presents. She finished off by popping a tiny teddy bear in to the top of each one, so that it peeked over the side.

Then she crept next door to Lisa's room. It was eerily quiet. She looked round quickly, trying to decide where to put the socks. If she dangled them at the end of each bed they'd be too easy to spot.

Under the pillows? Too obvious. On the bedside tables? No room. In the end, she decided to staple a piece of red ribbon to each sock to make a loop, and hung one on the end of each headboard. With any luck, Lisa and Alex might not even notice them until Christmas morning.

But as she leaned over Lisa's bed to attach the sock she slipped, and fell on to her pillow. Her face landed on something hard. It was an earring. A shiny, jet black earring – just like the ones Gudrun so often wore. Rachel looked closer. No, wait a moment – this *was* Gudrun's. It had to be.

Rachel's heart was beating fast as she made her way back to the party. What could it mean? Why had Gudrun left an earring on Lisa's pillow? She made up her mind that she would confront her – now, while she still had the nerve. Something was telling her that whatever the explanation, it was going to be important.

The first person she saw as she slipped back into the crowded party was Jason. He was standing alone, a drink in his hand, a dazed look on his face.

"Jason, I need to speak to Gudrun!" Rachel said urgently. "Do you know where she is?"

"She's gone," said Jason vacantly. Rachel noticed through her panic that his face was rather flushed, as if he'd had a little too much wine.

"Gone where?" she asked impatiently.

Jason shrugged. "I dunno," he slurred. "Just gone. We had dinner, and she said she had to go away in a hurry. She wanted me to cover for her in the chalet." He clapped his fist to his forehead.

"And I'm such a diphead, I said yes. I thought, you see, when she said she wanted to ask me something, I thought she wanted me. Me! So I said I'd do anything for her. Which wasn't very clever. Because now she's gone, and I don't even know where."

Rachel stared at him, her heart freezing over. Because suddenly, a horrible suspicion began to form in her mind, and she realized what she'd been too blind to see all along.

12

It was nearly midnight. The bright lights and happy laughter of the party contrasted sharply with the eerie quiet of the still, icy darkness outside. Rachel ploughed back up the hill to the apartment, her heart churning. She didn't understand what was happening – not then. She just knew that she was on the verge of an important discovery, and that it had everything to do with Gudrun.

She passed a group of carol singers bearing pretty lanterns, their faces shining as they strode past her, singing "Silent Night" in German as they went. The village church was thronging with worshippers, eagerly awaiting the first chimes of Christmas Day.

Once inside the apartment building Rachel made straight for Gudrun's door. It was unlocked. Too flustered to wonder why, she opened it and burst into the flat. It was obvious that Gudrun had left in a hurry. Her suitcase was gone, and most of her clothes. But, normally so fastidious, she had left her bed unmade and drawers half open; a trail of tights spilled out from one on to the floor. A torn piece of paper was jammed in another.

Rachel looked round wildly, her eyes focusing on the envelope. She tugged at the drawer until it sprang open, then pulled out a whole wodge of papers – bills, invoices, old letters. Impatiently, Rachel fumbled with the papers and tore the top one away from the others. She could see at once that it was a recent letter. As she began to read it her hand started to tremble and her eyes widened in incredulity. A wave of nausea washed over her but she forced herself to carry on reading, even though every phrase, every sentence, shot through her with an agonizing pain.

The letter was dated the 23rd December. It must have been posted just yesterday, although there didn't seem to be an envelope. The address was Jack's hotel in Grossburg. The single sheet had been typed on a word-processor, but the signature was unmistakable. Rachel would have recognized that bold, black, simple flourish anywhere.

Darling Gudrun,

It is impossible to put into words how much I miss you. Everywhere I go I see your fabulous face. Whenever I eat, I long for your exquisite cooking. And each time I go to bed I ache to feel you next to me.

Of course I can't risk coming to Edelweiss. She would make a terrible scene and all our magic would be destroyed. But I can't manage without you for much longer. So you'll just have to come here. I know it may be difficult to arrange but surely you can find someone to cover for you.

There's only one thing I want for Christmas, and that is to wake up and find you in my arms. Come quickly. The mistletoe is waiting.

> *With all my love*
> *Jack*

Her heart pounding, her eyes stinging with tears, Rachel sat on the bed and read and reread the letter. Wild thoughts and images raced round her head. She remembered those first, heady days when she and Jack had first got together, that summer in Spain.

"I did have a girlfriend," he'd told her, early on. "We were together for over a year and it was a messy break-up."

Rachel could recall the shadow that passed over his face as he spoke. She had been so happy there, wrapped in his arms under the Mediterranean stars, the sea lapping gently in the moonlight, that she had hardly registered that look of pain, or guilt – or was it regret?

"She's German," he'd told her. "We met when we were both repping in Turkey. After that, wherever the company sent me, she came too."

Rachel had felt vaguely alarmed when he said that. "But – you don't think I should do that, do you? I mean, I really like my job, and…"

"No, no," he'd reassured her tenderly. "Of course not. That's one of the things I love about you. You're so strong and independent. I'd hate you to give up your work for me. In fact, that was one of the things that went wrong…"

He'd fallen silent, remembering, and Rachel had not probed any further. For her, then, in the first throes of love, past girlfriends were an irrelevance.

But now, staring at the damning letter, she could hardly believe how stupid, how gullible she was. Of course, Gudrun must be the German girl he'd referred to. But judging by this, the affair was far from over.

She frowned, as she read it again. The letter was quite plainly from Jack. And yet, the phrases he used, the passion, were so very unlike him. With her, he was tender and affectionate, but never flowery or poetic. He was much more likely to tease her than flatter her. In fact, he was so unromantic he thought that films starring Meg Ryan were soppy. His idea of a loving gesture was to buy her a packet of Rolos occasionally.

It was as if she was reading the words of a stranger, thought Rachel. Mind you, she told herself mournfully, he could hardly have called her cooking exquisite. He once said her cheese on toast reminded him of his school gym shoes.

With another wave of horror, she realized that Gudrun must have known all along who Rachel was. Every time she smiled that supercilious smile, or whizzed past her on those flashy skis, she was probably laughing triumphantly to herself about the poor, deluded English girl. But why, when Jack was so clearly in love with her?

Rachel never liked to hang around fretting. Her response to a crisis was always to move into action. So there and then she made up her mind what she had to do. It was just a pity she'd have to wait until morning before she could put her plan into effect.

"Merry Christmas!" carolled Lisa the next morning, as she waltzed into Rachel's room bearing a tray of presents, coffee, champagne and little chocolates. But as soon as she set eyes on her friend, she stopped dead in her tracks.

"What on earth are you doing?" she demanded. Rachel was pulling her suitcase down from the top of the wardrobe, so fiercely that the wardrobe itself began to wobble dangerously.

Rachel looked up and forced herself to smile. "Oh, er – nothing. Happy Christmas. I was just getting ready to leave."

"What!" Lisa exclaimed. "Why?"

Silently, Rachel handed her Jack's letter. "I found this, last night, in Gudrun's room. Obviously that's where she's disappeared to. So I'm going too. I'm off to see them for myself."

Lisa read through the letter in amazement. "I just can't believe this. It certainly doesn't sound much like the Jack Woodford I know. Are you sure it's from him?"

Rachel nodded wearily. "It must be," she said. "I've thought and thought about it. He did tell me he'd had a German girlfriend. Only he said it was over. And that's definitely his signature, all right.

One thing's a bit odd, though. He's sent me quite a few letters, but never once typed on a word-processor. He always, always uses the same black fountain pen. Oh, I suppose it's because it's the one I gave him. For some reason he must have thought it would please me…"

"Maybe there's some simple explanation," suggested Lisa forlornly. "I mean – there could be a mistake, couldn't there?"

Rachel looked grim. "I don't see how. But whatever it is he thinks he's up to, I just need to confront him and get him to tell me himself what's going on. So listen – would you cover for me today, please? I'll do breakfast with the monkey club. Thank goodness Christmas lunch is at the Centre, so I might not even be missed. I'll try and get back by tomorrow, OK?"

Lisa nodded. "Of course – if it'll help. But can't you even try and enjoy a tiny bit of Christmas first? We don't have to be at the Chalet for another hour."

Rachel smiled a watery smile. "OK. And – thanks for this." She gestured at the tray. "I think I'll go for the champagne first. I don't normally drink alcohol for breakfast but this is kind of a special occasion."

"Hang on – I'll get Alex," said Lisa. "We're so excited about our stockings. How did you manage to get them into our room?"

"Last night – while you were at the party," Rachel explained. "I thought you two needed a little cheering up. How is everything?"

"Well, it has been a bit shaky, but we're fine this

morning. And we're so pleased with the stockings, we haven't even opened them yet. Tell you what, why don't we open them with you?"

A few minutes later Alex, Rachel and Lisa were sitting round the Christmas tree in the living room, toasting each other with champagne and orange juice. They were about to begin opening their presents when Lisa exclaimed: "No, wait – I must get a picture of this. Hang on!"

She disappeared into her room, and a few seconds later there was an anguished squeal. "My camera! It's disappeared!"

Rachel and Alex ran into her room and started to help her hunt for the little camera she was so fond of. "Do you think I could have left it in your room?" she asked Rachel dolefully.

"It's worth a look," shrugged Rachel. They crowded into her bedroom. There, on the bed, was the suitcase she'd just pulled down. The top had fallen open. And there, nestling in some tissue paper, just visible, was the camera.

All three of them stared at it, open-mouthed.

"But how – how did it get there?" stammered Lisa, barely able to look at Rachel.

"Look, I know there must be some explanation," said Alex. "But you were in Lisa's room last night, Rachel. Did you, er, borrow it or something?"

"Alex!" hissed Lisa, shocked.

"No, of course not," said Rachel slowly. "But I think I know how it found its way into my case. In fact, everything's suddenly falling into place."

She told them how she'd found Gudrun's earring on Lisa's bed the previous evening. How she'd rushed back to find her, only to discover she was too late.

"So I was right to think someone was trying to sabotage me," she finished. "Just completely wrong about who."

"But that's so horrible!" Lisa cried. "She must have been trying to make it look as if you were stealing from your best friend. As if she could have turned me against you!" She gave Rachel a quick hug. Then looked even more puzzled and added, "But why would anyone do something so mean? It doesn't make sense."

"It does if she thought I was trying to steal her boyfriend away," said Rachel. "At least, I suppose that's what she must have thought. Only, judging by that letter, she doesn't seem to have much to worry about."

Alex was reading the letter now, squinting over the words. "I hope you don't expect me to write things like this," he said to Lisa. "I mean – what bloke would come out with stuff like this? I don't think Jack could have written it, Rachel."

"I hope you're right," Rachel told him. "Frankly, I think there must be a side to Jack that none of us has ever seen, not even me. That's why I have to see him with Gudrun and find out the truth."

Breakfast at Red Chalet was one long agony for Rachel. She forced herself to look cheerful as she handed each guest a special gift and wished them a very merry Christmas. The worst of it was that they all, for once, looked so happy. Janet and Sean were holding hands, and she was wearing a beautiful velvet scarf – obviously a very special present from her husband. Laura and Mike were pulling crackers and reading out silly jokes. Brett was stroking Nina's hand, which now sported a large, handsome diamond on one finger. Jonquil, looking as glamorous as ever in a swathe of green and purple silk, had obviously decided to be gracious.

"Oh, darling, how lovely!" she exclaimed, opening the little box of marzipan fruit which Rachel had given her. "And here's something for you – just to show you that all is forgiven." Rachel gasped as she unwrapped a delicate pair of snowflake earrings.

"Well, you did seem to appreciate them," said Jonquil. "And you do really work so hard for us."

"Hear, hear," agreed Sean. And Janet grinned, and echoed him.

"Yeah, hooray for Rachel!"

And as everyone hugged her and wished her a happy Christmas, Rachel felt the tears pricking her eyelids. Somehow, these ten disparate people who had made her life so difficult for so long had turned into a family – her family. And just as everything had got so warm and welcoming, she was going to have to desert them.

The telephone rang and Michael went to answer it. "It's for Brett!" he called from the hallway.

Brett disappeared for a few minutes. When he returned his face was set and drawn. Without even glancing at Nina he announced: "It's my wife, Cerise. I've got to go to her at once. It seems that – well, she's about to have a baby. My baby."

13

There was a shocked silence after Brett delivered his bombshell. Then everything began to rush by like a speeded-up video. Brett slammed out of the door with Jonquil close behind him. Her loud, complaining voice rang down the stairs as she asked a series of tactless questions which he seemed to have no intention of answering.

"How on earth could Cerise be pregnant? I spoke to her on the phone a couple of months ago and she certainly didn't mention it then, so how do you know she's telling the truth? I mean, you haven't even seen her for, let's see, at least six months. Come to think of it, how do you know it's yours at all? And if you're going, what's going to happen to the Barbie Doll? We'll be lumbered, I suppose – big sister bailing out little brother as per usual?"

Nina sat composedly at the breakfast table. The diamond flashed on her finger as she stirred her coffee. She seemed remarkably unconcerned at Brett's announcement, and didn't even react as Jonquil's brittle words echoed through the room. She made no move to follow them. Rachel couldn't help admiring her cool.

There was a loud rap on the front door. Rachel opened it to reveal a tall figure in an enormous overcoat and a handsome fake-fur hat, his arms full of roses.

"Merry Christmas, Rachel," beamed Karl as he handed them to her. "I have brought you these. And – wait one moment." He shuffled through his pockets and drew out a package which he thrust into her free hand.

Bewildered, Rachel made way for him to come in. He grinned round at the hushed company still at breakfast and poured himself a cup of coffee. "And a merry Christmas to all of you. I am not intruding?" It was more like a statement than a question. Karl never worried too much about formalities.

Rachel opened the package to reveal a brightly-coloured knitted scarf. "Oh, Karl, it's beautiful," she said, genuinely pleased. "But whenever did you find time to knit it?"

Karl frowned, puzzled. "No, me? Of course not. I bought it in Edelweiss." Rachel sighed. Jack would have known she was joking. Jack would have had some ready answer like he always did. With a jolt, she remembered that probably they would never joke together again. But still, she was determined to go and find him.

One by one, the rest of the chalet group found

excuses to leave the room. When they were alone, Rachel turned to Karl.

"I'm sorry," she said, "I really am. I love the scarf. And I did enjoy our, er, time together the other day. But I can't see you again, Karl. I – I have to go away." And then she found herself blurting out the truth – about Jack, about the discovery of the letter, then the camera, and her suspicions about Gudrun.

Sobbing, now, she gulped: "So you see, Karl, I have to go now, today. I have to get the train and go and find them..."

Karl gently removed the flowers from her arms, sat down and hugged her. "I understand," he consoled her. "At least you can be pleased about one thing. It seems you were not inventing a villain at all. It sounds to me as though you may have been proved right."

"I never thought about it like that," admitted Rachel. "Oh, Karl! You are nice. I wish I was in love with you instead."

At that moment Brett burst into the dining room, his face grim. "Rachel, I have to make the first plane I can get to London," he announced briskly. "So do you know the times of trains to the airport? Can you arrange to get me there?"

Before Rachel had a chance to reply, Karl said firmly: "It is Christmas Day. There is no transport today to the train station. There is one train for you in twenty minutes. I will drive you there." He turned to Rachel. "And I will have to take you a little further, for your connection to Grossburg."

* * *

It was a nightmare journey. Karl drove her all the way to Amadeus, about twenty miles from Edelweiss, and saw her on to the train. Rachel found it difficult to tear herself away from his huge, bear-like embrace. He was such a strong, reassuring sort of man. For one instant, she thought about forgetting the whole impulse. She could stay here, with Karl. He'd drive her back to Edelweiss, make a fuss of her, share Christmas dinner with her. Maybe even invite her into his hot tub again...

But there was a far more insistent need that drove her to pull away from him and walk on to the icy platform without even turning back to wave goodbye. This was a mission, and one that only she could undertake.

The train seemed to be stuck at Amadeus for hours. No one seemed to be able to tell her why. Rachel was cold, miserable and uncomfortable. But when it finally pulled out of the station at eleven o'clock she cheered up. On the way at last! Grossburg was only about sixty miles from here. She might even make it by lunchtime!

It wasn't long before she realized how wrong she was. This was the one and only train on that route and it stopped at every little village along the track. There were long, inexplicable delays every half hour or so. Once, it was something to do with snow piled on the tracks. Another time, they had to wait for a family with six very elderly relatives, all of whom mounted the train very, very slowly. And then, when they were all settled, the driver, who turned out to be another relative, insisted on coming into the carriage to wish them all a merry Christmas.

Worst of all, for Rachel, were the reunions on platforms – the passionate embraces of lovers who were meeting again after a long parting; loving couples hugging and smiling – just as she and Jack should have been.

It was mid-afternoon by the time Rachel found herself standing at Grossburg station, waiting for a taxi. Of course – it was Christmas Day. No wonder there was no one around. In the end, she hailed a horse and carriage – obviously there for the tourists. She felt slightly ridiculous sitting in the open carriage in the freezing wind as they trotted along slippery, ice-covered roads.

It was not long before Rachel was standing uncertainly in the lobby of the Hotel Lisbeth. It seemed very smart, smelling of cigars and expensive perfume. There was a huge, glittering Christmas tree in the middle of the room. Fashionably dressed skiers were bustling past, anxious to get in a little session on the slopes before the evening feast.

Rachel made her way over to the reception desk. A pleasant-looking girl smiled enquiringly at her. "Could you tell me where I might find Jack Woodford?" Rachel asked.

"Jack? Oh, he should be around somewhere," said the girl, obviously English. "We've been so busy here, you wouldn't believe. One minute we're full. Then two rooms are cancelled. Then the guests turn up after all. Then we're overbooked. He hasn't had a minute to himself, none of us has.

Hang on, I'll see if he's in his office. It's just over there, second door along. Oh, wait a minute. Oh, dear."

The girl looked embarrassed as she stared at the door of the office. Rachel followed her gaze. And froze. There, coming out and walking across the lobby, was Gudrun. She was wearing a very short, very tight red skirt and an even tighter top. The buttons had obviously been hastily done up, because they were all askew. Her hair, immaculate as ever, shimmered down her back. Her face wore a satisfied smile that made Rachel want to smash her teeth in.

But, somehow, she couldn't follow her or call out after her. She couldn't even move, but just stood rooted to the spot as Gudrun, unaware, sashayed right across the lobby and disappeared through another door.

Stricken, Rachel turned to the friendly receptionist. She had a sympathetic look on her face and seemed about to say something. But Rachel wasn't going to hang around to hear it. Suddenly, she knew she couldn't go through with this. She couldn't just march into Jack's office and demand to know what was going on. It was just going to be too painful.

Instead, she thrust her suitcase into the arms of the surprised girl. "Look after it, please," she said urgently. "I – I have to go now!" And then she turned on her heel and rushed headlong out of the hotel, into the bleak, grey, frozen air.

Not thinking about where she was going, she charged along the unfamiliar roads, slithering into treacherous patches of ice until she reached what looked like the main drag. The town was much larger than Edelweiss with cafés and restaurants crowded along one strip, all full of holiday-makers enjoying coffee and cakes. Couples with skis balanced on their shoulders wandered along hand in hand, looking surprised as Rachel charged past them, hardly aware of them in her determination to get away from the awful humiliation of what she had just seen.

Racing faster and faster along the street, she suddenly hit an unexpected patch of hard ice. Completely out of control, she hurtled along, skidded, and landed bang into the arms of a familiar figure in black, with a blue and white scarf. The colours of his home team.

It was Jack. Dear, sweet Jack, wearing the scarf that she'd knitted him. In those few moments, her relief turned to fury. How could he? she wondered, through the fog of emotion and panic. How could he still be wearing that, after he'd betrayed her?

Jack held her tight to steady her. It was only when she was upright that he stood back, looked at her properly, and realized who she was. And then his face broke into a smile of genuine delight.

"Rachel!" he exclaimed. "Darling – how wonderful! This is the best, easily the best Christmas present you could possibly have given me. But – but how did you manage it? Oh, I can't believe it's really you!"

And then he was pulling her into his arms and kissing her – a long, passionate kiss, a mixture of tenderness and deep, deep longing. For a few moments, Rachel allowed herself to sink into the warmth, the wonderful sensation of being with Jack again, of being loved by him.

Then she remembered all that had happened, and anger took over once again. "Look – I think I deserve an explanation," she said. "Jack – are you completely crazy, or is it me?"

Jack gave her a long, searching look. Eventually, he said: "I'm not quite sure what you mean, love. But maybe we have got some sorting out to do. Come on, let me buy you the best hot chocolate you've ever had in your life."

Half an hour later, warmed with the delicious chocolate, and feeling even warmer now that Jack was clasping her hand, Rachel was almost bursting with happiness. *It's OK, after all!* she kept telling herself. *Jack loves me! He loves me! It's me he loves!*

"Of course I love you," Jack told her, shocked that she could ever have doubted him. "Maybe I should have told you more about Gudrun. But there never seemed much point. I told you when I met you that it was all over between us. We'd broken up ages ago. Gudrun took it a bit hard and she did keep writing, and ringing, trying to get me to see her." He sighed. "Occasionally she'd turn up out of the blue and beg me to give it another try. Come to think of it, she only started doing that when I told her I'd met you. But ever since I got this job, I hadn't seen her. I thought she'd finally accepted that it was over. Until yesterday..."

"Go on," Rachel urged, hope beginning to stir in

her heart. "What happened yesterday?"

Jack looked troubled. "Well, it was very strange," he said. "Like I said, I hadn't seen her for ages, hadn't even heard from her."

"So you didn't realize she'd got a job with Dream Ticket?" breathed Rachel.

"No idea," admitted Jack. "She could easily have done that under a different name. It never crossed my mind... And then yesterday she showed up and announced she'd come for Christmas. Just as if we were still a couple. She kept saying how much she'd missed me and how much better it used to be when she didn't have to work away from me. It was quite weird, actually. I tried to tell her she couldn't stay, but..." Now he looked even more troubled.

"Well, she cried a lot, got hysterical. She said she had nowhere to go for Christmas. So I said she could stay in my room just for the night. I camped out in the office. I've been more or less living there anyway – we've had so much trouble here with our bookings."

"I – I thought you were making excuses," put in Rachel lamely. "It was so horrible, Jack. Everything was going wrong for me, and then I started to think you'd stopped loving me. And then I found your letter..."

"What letter?" Jack was clearly puzzled.

"The one to Gudrun," Rachel explained patiently, still not quite sure that everything had been cleared up. "The one where you invited her to spend Christmas with you."

"Rachel, this is serious," said Jack. "I didn't

write any letter to Gudrun. Of course I didn't. I think she must have written it herself. And that's not the only letter she's been writing. I stayed up all last night, studying those cancellations that have been driving us all round the bend. I knew there was something bogus about them. I'm fairly sure she sent those – God knows why. I suppose she was just trying to create chaos, to make sure I'd be stuck here over Christmas. That's really sick."

"That's not all," said Rachel slowly. "I've just realized something else. When I went into Gudrun's room last night, the door was unlocked. The letter was just crying out to be read. I think she intended me to find it. She even wanted me to follow her here. You know what, Jack. It sounds crazy, but I really think she believes you two are still together, and that I'm the evil one, trying to steal you away."

Arm in arm they made their way along the darkening street. The little cafés were closing down now, and there were very few people around. Everyone was preparing for Christmas night. In the distance, the bells of a little church pealed joyfully, and from somewhere in the hills came the sound of carols.

It was beginning to snow, but Rachel had never in her life felt so warm. Her heart was blazing. Everything was coming right again. All her nightmares were fading away. Jack loved her. It was Christmas. She was so happy she wanted to burst.

Soon, they reached a picturesque lake, surrounded by fir trees. A pale moon was hovering in the sky, reflected on the glinting ice. But it disappeared as the snow fell thicker in huge, soft flakes. Jack turned to her and gazed into her face for a long time. Then he said, very seriously, "I'm so sorry, darling. I can't bear to think of how much this has hurt you. But right now, I just feel so happy that you're here."

He pulled her towards him in a long, tender kiss, their lips hot and hungry despite the blizzard gathering round them. Dreamily she opened her eyes, not wanting to end the magic of that kiss, these precious moments with Jack. And then, as if with a sixth sense, she became aware of another presence somewhere nearby. She focused on a tree behind Jack's shoulder. Surely there was a shadow, moving. Then it disappeared. Then came into view again.

Suddenly a blood-curdling scream pierced the air. The shadow was real. A real woman came running from behind the tree. It was Gudrun. The screams were Gudrun's screams, raiding the still-ness as she rushed past them and threw herself headlong into the frozen lake. There was a crash, a shower of splinters, then a final deathly screech as she disappeared through the shattered ice.

14

"Merry Christmas!" called Karl, in a deep, rousing voice. "Raise your glasses with me, my friends, and let us all drink to this special day."

Everyone dutifully raised their glasses. Everyone drank and murmured, "Merry Christmas." But no one was looking very merry. In fact, "Gloomy Christmas" would have been a more accurate description, Lisa thought as she glanced round the little bar.

For once, the only remotely happy face seemed to belong to Janet, who sat snuggled in a corner with Sean, her face glowing. Laura and Mike were with them, and they were smiling and talking as usual. But the happiness stopped there.

Jonquil sat hunched next to a worried-looking Tommy. Her face was strained, her fingers drumming nervously on the table. "I wish Rachel was here," she announced unexpectedly. "Everything would be so much better if she was."

"Hear, hear!" clamoured Janet and Sean. "We want Rachel, we want Rachel."

"Ah, yes, well, many of us want the delectable Rachel," Karl said heartily. "But she is not here, as you can see. And knowing you would be devastated without your alluring hostess, I thought the least I could do was invite you for this lunchtime drink and snack. So let us drink to our absent friend."

As everyone solemnly clinked glasses again, Jason looked up miserably from where he sat slumped against Lisa. "Absent friends," he corrected. "Rachel's not the only alluring hostess that seems to have gone missing. Let's have a toast to absent women."

Alex patted him on the back. "Know how you feel," he mumbled. "It's been like that for weeks with me." He looked up at Lisa and grinned. "But it's worth it when you're together again, isn't it?"

Lisa smiled weakly, and clinked her glass with his and then with Jason's. "Oh, definitely," she said, trying to sound more convincing than she felt. Of course, it was lovely being with Alex again. Of course she still loved him. But why was there this niggling doubt fluttering round her heart? Why was she looking at him, now, as though he were a stranger – a rather awkward, rather shabby stranger?

The answer, of course, was standing at the bar, draining a glass of hot cider and laughing with Karl. Jean-Pierre was looking even more devastatingly handsome than usual, and although she hated herself for doing it, Lisa couldn't help comparing his rugged good looks and easy elegance with sweet, shambling Alex, who never much cared whether his socks matched, and who actually preferred to wear old clothes because they were more comfortable and didn't show the dirt.

For a moment, Jean-Pierre's eyes met hers. Quickly she shifted her gaze away, and looked instead at a lone figure, quietly sipping a glass of wine. "Nina!" called Lisa. "Come and join us! Do!"

Nina smiled and sat in the chair next to Jason. "How are you?" Lisa asked. "It must be rotten for you – Brett disappearing like that. Are you terribly upset?"

Nina shrugged. "Not really. He was getting on my nerves, really. It was OK at first, but he was really intense most of the time. Not much fun to be with. And you can imagine what it was like with both of them." She indicated Jonquil, a few tables away, now holding forth loudly and piercingly about other, better Christmasses she had known.

"But – but you always looked so happy together," protested Lisa, shocked.

"Yeah, well, there you go," said Nina. "We weren't."

Lisa still couldn't quite believe her. "But what about that fabulous ring?" she demanded, staring at the huge diamond flashing on Nina's finger.

"Oh, I love the diamond," said Nina, looking at it fondly. "But that doesn't mean I love the man. Actually, it doesn't mean he loves me, either. In fact, it was when he gave it to me that I really knew something was up."

"How?" That was Jason, Alex and Lisa all together, all intrigued.

"Haven't you ever noticed?" Nina asked them, clearly rather amused at their incredulity. "The bigger the present the bigger the guilt. I think Brett was cooling off just as much as I was. His wife's done me a favour, really. Although I can't say I'm sure she's doing him one. I mean, he's going to have to go back to her now, isn't he?"

Alex looked thoughtful. "Aren't you glad I only gave you modest little Christmas presents this year?" he said at last to Lisa. "A jumper, a scarf, a pair of ear muffs. That just goes to show how much I'm not cooling off."

Lisa grinned at him, suddenly feeling affectionate again. "You didn't mention the black silky underwear. Doesn't that count as an extravagant present?" She looked at him quizzically for a moment, then added: "Oh, no, of course not. That was really a present for you, wasn't it?"

At that moment Tammy came bursting through the door of the bar. "Hi everyone!" she greeted them cheerily. "Merry Christmas! Karl said he'd invited you all along. I've only just managed to get away." She pulled a funny face. "In our hotel we have to do a children's party. It's really gruesome. Hey! Where's Rachel?" She looked round, puzzled. "And where's Gudrun?"

Lisa leapt up. "Let's find you another chair, shall we!" she said. Then, away from Jason, she hissed: "Gudrun's disappeared, Jason doesn't know where. But Rachel thinks she's gone to see

Jack, Rachel's boyfriend. So Rachel's gone after them. And you get the prize for making the most number of boobs in one go."

Tammy tried to look concerned. But she couldn't help feeling a sudden warm glimmer of hope. "Really?" she said. "You mean – Jason's here and Gudrun isn't?" Lisa stared at her, amused but disapproving at the same time. "I mean, poor Rachel," Tammy corrected herself hurriedly. "Here, I've brought a load of crackers for everyone. We might as well pull them now. Jason – hey, Jason. Fancy making a bang with me?"

For a split second after Gudrun had plunged, screeching, through the ice into the lake, Jack and Rachel had stared at each other in horror. Then, both of them charged into action. "Wait here and watch for her to come up!" Jack ordered. "I'm going to the First Aid cabin." He raced off to a wooden cabin a little way away, and a couple of minutes later was back, dragging a ladder.

"She's bobbed to the surface," Rachel reported. "Let's hope she managed to get some air. I think she's gone under again."

The old, wooden ladder had been collapsed like a telescope. Now Jack was tearing at the hinges on either side, while Rachel pulled it to its full length. Even in the panic and terror of those terrible seconds, she was remembering a similar crisis, last summer, when she and Jack had worked together to save the life of a girl who had fallen down a cliff. *Let's hope we'll be able to pull it off again*, she thought fervently.

Jack extended the ladder over the lake to the place where Gudrun had fallen through the ice. "Let's hope she's strong enough to see it and grab it," he muttered.

"She won't be," said Rachel firmly. "Look – you know what we've got to do. You'll just have to lean on the ladder with all your weight, and I'll crawl along it and see if I can pull her out."

Jack looked unconvinced. "I can't let you, Rachel," he protested. "It's too dangerous. What if I can't support the ladder? What if you fall in as well?"

"It's her only chance, Jack!" Rachel said urgently. "We can't afford to waste any time. Come on – now!"

His face troubled, Jack said nothing more. He did as Rachel had suggested, lying down over the end of the ladder that was balanced at the edge of the lake. At once, Rachel began to crawl along the rungs, over the frozen water.

"How are you doing?" Jack's voice echoed eerily across the darkening sky.

"OK," called back Rachel, trying to keep her voice steady. She was making her way steadily along the ladder, forcing herself to concentrate on each rung, thinking only about reaching the next one, and the next. She was dimly aware that it was cold, very cold. So cold that her knees and her toes were beginning to ache. But still she crawled further and further into the middle of the lake, to the spot where Gudrun had disappeared.

At last, weary now and so cold she could barely move, she was within inches of the shattered ice.

With a jolt of relief, Rachel caught a glimpse of a head in the water, then a hand, then a clump of matted hair. Gudrun was there, surely she was within her reach. All she had to do was find a way to bridge those few inches.

Rachel knelt on the edge of the ladder and peered down. "Gudrun!" she called. "Gudrun – can you hear me? Can you try and reach me?"

There was a response, of sorts – a gurgling of water as the drowning girl turned to the sound of Rachel's voice, her hands grabbing at the ice around her. But wherever she grabbed, the ice would give way and shatter into the water.

Rachel thought fast. "It's OK, Gudrun – it's OK. I'm coming!" she called, with more confidence than she felt.

Now she was lying full length on the ladder. That way, she calculated, there would be less strain at the other end. Flat on her stomach, she edged carefully towards the end of the ladder, her arms outstretched. She was getting closer, closer to the flailing, spluttering figure in the water. But still, she couldn't quite reach the girl, and it was all Gudrun could do to remain afloat, scrabbling vainly for something she could clutch that wouldn't melt away in her hand.

Rachel had one more idea. Now she was lying sideways on the ladder. The new angle gave her just the leverage she needed to reach further, then further towards the struggling girl. Gudrun made one mighty effort and flung one arm towards Rachel. At the same moment Rachel lunged out, desperately, and grasped her arm. With a surge of triumph, she pulled with all her strength. She needed her other arm, but didn't dare let go of the ladder.

For a few seconds nothing happened. Rachel clung with one hand to the ladder, the other to Gudrun's wrist. Then the ladder began to move and, almost without protest, Rachel felt herself slipping off. But still, her hand was hanging on to the last rung, as the ladder began to pull away and back to the shore.

Rachel never really knew afterwards how she survived those next nightmare moments. All she was aware of was a sensation of being torn apart as the ladder pulled her back across the frozen lake, and she in turn dragged the near lifeless body behind her.

Minutes later, two strong arms were lifting her to the safety of the shore. Jack was cradling her in his arms, whispering her name, pleading with her to speak to him. "Where – where's Gudrun?" she murmured. Then she looked up and saw that an ambulance had arrived, and Gudrun was being given the kiss of life.

One moment, she was lying still in the snow. The next, she was coughing and spluttering and spewing out water. After a few minutes, she sat up wildly and stared at Jack and Rachel. Even now, her face was twisted with hate.

"Mine!" she announced in a deathly voice. "He's mine! All mine!"

Somehow, all three of them were bundled into an ambulance, wrapped in blankets. Gudrun was plainly very sick, and the moment they arrived at the hospital she was rushed into Casualty. The ambulance driver tossed a soaking black bag at Rachel. "The lady's handbag – someone should look after it," he said in German.

The next couple of hours seemed to go in slow motion. Rachel was examined by a doctor, then left in a bed for a while, then examined again. Eventually a kind-looking nurse brought her a steaming cup of soup. "Not exactly a Christmas feast, is it love?" she said sympathetically in German. Rachel smiled gratefully, happy to be warm and safe.

After another long while, the doctor examined her again and pronounced her fit enough to get dressed and go home. Jack appeared, looking solicitous and carrying her suitcase. "You needed some dry clothes," he explained. "So I had your suitcase sent from the hotel."

He came and sat down next to her and took her hand. "Another dramatic rescue for the intrepid duo," he said, trying to make a joke.

"Yeah, but a bit more near-death this time," answered Rachel, still feeling shaken. "How is Gudrun, do you know?"

Jack looked grave. "Well, they seem to think she'll live," he replied. "But they want me to hang around because she's not off the danger list yet. Oh, my darling, I can't tell you how sorry I am about this – this mess! You shouldn't have had to get involved ... I had no idea, you see. I never even thought she'd turn up like that. But she's obsessed – deranged. She's not safe, Rachel. She doesn't seem to know what she's doing any more.

I know it looked as though she was trying to kill herself and maybe she was. But you know, it's just as likely that she was trying to push you into the lake. Remember how she hurtled past us? She could easily have been aiming at you and then skidded, lost control, and fell in herself. Whatever was on her mind, I'll never forgive myself for letting her anywhere near you."

"Well it's hardly your fault," Rachel reasoned. "But I wish you'd told me about her, Jack – properly, I mean. If only I'd realized…"

Jack gazed at her intently. "I know. I should have explained. But you see, it had all become such a mess. Gudrun was throwing these terrible jealous rages, all I wanted was to get her out of my life. Then you came along and it was my chance to start again. I just wanted to forget all about her, and the nasty, ugly way it all ended."

"I suppose that if you love someone, you want to love all of them," said Rachel gently. "Not just the bits they want you to see, but everything. Knowing about Gudrun doesn't make me love you any less. But it sort of hurts that you didn't trust me enough to tell me about her."

"I know!" Jack said earnestly. "I can see that now. I'll make it up to you, Rachel, I promise." His face brightened. "But listen – at least we'll get to spend Christmas together. Why don't you go back to the hotel now, and I'll join you later, when Gudrun's settled. They probably won't want me to stay more than another hour or two."

It wasn't until Rachel was tucked into a taxi and on her way back to the hotel that she realized that as well as her own handbag and suitcase, she was clutching something else. Something black, and heavy, and still slightly damp. Gudrun's bag. Idly, she opened it, wondering if it contained any papers or documents they might need at the hospital. But as she scrabbled further into the bag, her eyes widened with renewed shock.

She tapped the driver urgently on the shoulder. "I've changed my mind!" she announced. "Take me to the station!"

15

Rachel was panting heavily, her heart pounding fast, as the train pulled away from Grossburg Station. She had known that the last train would be leaving at ten o'clock and she'd only just managed to catch it. It was only now, as she gazed out at the dark, frozen landscape rushing by, that she had time to reflect on the extraordinary events of the day and her final discovery.

She was alone in the carriage. Who else, after all, would be travelling through the mountains late in the evening on Christmas night? So she spread her things out, and then settled down to examine the contents of Gudrun's bag.

Buried right at the bottom, in a little velvet pouch, were Jonquil's missing designs – the musical sequence of brooches and earrings she'd been hoping to sell to her fancy buyer.

It was when she'd seen those that Rachel had made up her mind to go all out to catch the train and get back to Edelweiss by the next morning.

She'd remembered that that was when Jonquil was meeting the client who was coming all the way from Switzerland to look at her designs. Rachel felt a pang of remorse when she thought of Jack. How would he react when he finally returned to the hotel, to find she'd disappeared? There hadn't even been time to leave him a note.

Then Rachel fingered the beautiful, strange designs once again. Of course she had to do her best to get them back to Jonquil. She had no doubt about that. But how did they come to be in Gudrun's bag at all? How had she managed to orchestrate everything so that all the suspicion fell on Rachel?

She scrabbled further into the bag – out came a hairbrush, some letters, a purse, an earring ... Rachel recognized it at once. It was jet black, very distinctive. Just like the one she had found on Lisa's pillow the previous evening. Could it really be only twenty-four hours since she'd made that discovery? To Rachel, it felt like a whole lifetime.

Right at the bottom of the bag her fingers closed round a hard, metallic object. Even before she looked at it, she knew what it would be. It was Jason's precious key-ring, silver, with an ace of hearts design. So Gudrun had taken that, as well – and again suspicion had fallen on Rachel.

Over the long, bumpy journey, with endless stops at little mountain villages, and long hold-ups where freezing snow was blocking the rail tracks, Rachel sat staring out of the window, deep in thought.

First, she cast her mind back to the day Jonquil had discovered her most precious designs were missing. Rachel remembered how Marjorie, then the police, had interrogated her. How she'd admitted that she'd cleaned the chalet rooms that day because Heidi was ill. But wait!

Had Heidi really been ill that morning? She concentrated hard, and Heidi's words wafted back into her consciousness. "I got the message that I wasn't needed." Now, why hadn't that struck anyone as strange? In a flash, Rachel realized what had happened. It was Gudrun who'd phoned and told Heidi she wasn't needed. That way, she'd have the chance to sneak in and take the jewellery. And, conveniently, it would mean Rachel would have to do the rooms – and that would make it look as though she'd had the perfect opportunity to steal from Jonquil's bedroom.

Then everything – all her half-formed suspicions and doubts – began to slide into place. Gudrun had known who Rachel was all along. She must have got the job with Dream Ticket so that she could be near her, and plan her downfall. If that was the case, then Gudrun could have been responsible for all the accidents and mishaps that had dogged Rachel.

She remembered Janet's boots – she had been so sure that she'd fitted them carefully. Could Gudrun have deliberately changed them? Thinking carefully, Rachel remembered how envious she'd been, that first morning, at the efficiency of the German girl working beside her. Yes, it fitted! Gudrun was right there, next to her.

She had even been round to the chalet the day that Rachel's cake had so disastrously burned.

Rachel almost squeaked aloud, realizing how easy it must have been for Gudrun to have slipped back into the kitchen while Rachel was with Lisa and Nina that afternoon...

Feeling slightly sick, by now, Rachel began to see what must have been happening. What had begun as small mishaps – little more than pranks, really – had started to grow. They'd become more serious, and more dangerous, too. *Could Gudrun have been responsible for Janet's accident on the toboggan?* she wondered fearfully.

She thought back again to the events of that day. It had been snowing, so everyone had piled into Northern Heights. Rachel and Lisa had worked together, pulling the toboggans out of the storage cupboard. She remembered checking each one very carefully – that was why she had been so puzzled, later, to discover that Janet's had had such a major fault.

Wait! Gudrun had been there! She recalled how Gudrun had arrived with her very active, sporty party who had wanted special cross-country tips for their boots. Gudrun had suggested using the red toboggans. Could she have tampered with one of them? Rachel was beginning to be more and more sure that Gudrun was capable of anything...

Her fingers closed once again on the little embossed key-ring. Why would Gudrun have taken that? Then Rachel remembered how, desperate for someone to help her out with her cake disaster, she'd rushed to find Jason and begged him to share some of the pastries he'd made with Gudrun.

Gudrun must have followed her there – must

have known, once again, that suspicion would fall on her if Jason lost something that day. And of course Gudrun would have had every opportunity to take his key-ring. After all, by then they'd started to spend so much time together...

Rachel shivered involuntarily. It was horrible to think how closely Gudrun must have been watching her and following her. And even more horrible to realize how viciously she hated her.

But it seemed even worse, somehow, that she'd take something from Jason – who was so crazy about her. Rachel wondered if Gudrun had had any feelings for him at all. Or whether she'd just been using him. Even now, he was covering for her, taking care of her chalet, while she had rushed off to meet the man she really loved.

With a shudder, Rachel wondered if that was true. Did Gudrun love Jack? Is that why she'd constructed such a catalogue of misery and disaster? Somehow, it seemed much more likely that she was not capable of love – not real love. Just passion, and jealousy and deep, deep despair...

"Why do men always have to be so competitive?" Lisa asked Tammy, despairingly. Karl's bar was buzzing. The windows had all steamed up in the heat and the hubbub of the crowded room. Jean-Pierre and Alex had played two games of snooker and won one each. Now they were arm wrestling, egged on by the rest of the crowd.

"Oh, they're not all," replied Tammy, knowingly. "Jean-Pierre's like that because of being a Scorpio,

I expect. I mean, he's typical, isn't he? I bet your Alex is one as well, isn't he? No? Well, I suppose he wouldn't be. He's far too gentle. What then? Aries? No, they're not competitive at all. Jason, what sign are you?"

Jason looked up morosely. "Aries, I think."

Tammy beamed triumphantly. "There! What did I tell you, Lisa! He's got Aries written all over him."

"What does that say about me, then?" asked Jason. "That I'm a pathetic dupe, or merely an idiot?"

Tammy smiled at him fondly. "Oh, nothing like that," she assured him. "Just that you're a very sensitive person and that can make you vulnerable. Unless, of course, you hang around with earthy types like me. I'm a Gemini, you see, so I can appreciate your watery nature without trying to dry it all out."

Still gazing at the arm wrestling, Lisa frowned. "I don't think it's very healthy sitting round here," she declared. "I think those two are going to start biting each other's tails unless we get some fresh air and exercise."

"Especially as there's the big Christmas feast tonight," agreed Nina, watching the match with amused detachment.

"How about snow-boarding?" suggested Tammy.

"Great idea!" agreed Lisa at once. "Hey – you two. Let go of each other's wrists. I declare the match a draw, for what it's worth. Let's get out on to the slopes!"

Everyone trudged back to Northern Heights for snow-boards. Everyone, that is, except for Nina.

"I'm not sure I can be bothered," she said to Karl.

"Oh, but you would enjoy it," he told her. "Come with me. I have snow-boards. I will teach you, yes? I think you perhaps need a little diversion outdoors."

Once they were out on the nursery slopes, Lisa couldn't help feeling rather impressed with Alex. Not only did he manage to stay upright on his glossy black board as he skittered down the slopes – he actually performed a few quite tricky manoeuvres: a jump, a double jump, a fancy turn and then a twist.

At least, she was impressed until the inevitable athletic figure, dressed in black with neon stripes, whizzed round them in a series of corkscrews. It was, of course, Jean-Pierre, master of the slopes, effortlessly outshining all of them as he flew through the snow, barely touching the board beneath him.

"Hey, I was watching you," he said, giving Alex a friendly punch on the back. Alex tried not to cough too much at the impact of Jean-Pierre's hearty slap. "No, but you have a good style, I think," Jean-Pierre added.

"Thanks," muttered Alex. "I just sort of treat it like a skateboard. I was always great on that. Mainly because I wasn't allowed roller-blades."

Tammy and Lisa laughed at his throw-away remark, but Jean-Pierre merely looked baffled. He obviously didn't understand modesty.

"Oh, no, it is much different from skateboarding," he told Alex seriously. "Look, why don't we go up higher and I will show you. You see – once you are

157

on a proper slope you will see what a much finer sport it is, in the snow."

With a shrug, Alex followed him up the next slope, and up the next, to the steepest nursery slope. The rest of the crowd straggled behind. Some wanted to watch. Others were happy slithering around on the smaller slopes. Tammy was showing Jason her preferred style – sliding along on her stomach. Karl seemed to have taken charge of Nina. He stood at the bottom of the slope waiting to catch her as she careered down it.

Lisa anxiously plodded after Alex and Jean-Pierre. When they reached the top of the steep slope, Jean-Pierre turned to Alex. "You see – a much better slope for snow-boarding. The rest – it is fun for beginners. But you and I – we need something more manly, no?"

With an expert flourish, Jean-Pierre leapt in the air, landed on his board, and flew down the slope leaving showers of ice behind him as he descended. When he reached the bottom he chopped the board smartly to a halt, jumped off and turned round to face Alex and Lisa. He folded his arms and looked up expectantly.

"Alex," said Lisa nervously. "If you've never done this, I don't think you—"

But it was too late. With a determined jutting of his jaw, Alex had leapt on to his snow-board, just as Jean-Pierre had done, and was rushing down the slope, faster and faster, and faster still until he was completely out of control. Somehow, the board snagged against some hard lump hidden by the snow. It bounced, jerked, careered into a mad skid, and Alex was thrown off.

For a couple of seconds he seemed to be flying in the air. Then he landed in the snow, his leg splayed awkwardly beneath him. He was completely still.

"Alex!" screamed Lisa. "Alex!" She rushed down the hill, flung herself to the ground beside him, held his cold hands in hers, and willed him to open his eyes. "Alex – say you can hear me!" she begged. "Tell me you're OK!"

16

When Rachel appeared at breakfast the next
morning she was amazed at her reception.
The whole chalet broke into cheers and applause.
"Rachel's back!" exclaimed Jonquil, which amazed
her even more. "Now everything will be all right
again. Rachel, darling, you wouldn't believe how
ghastly it's been without you!"

"Yes, we've missed you ever so much, Rachel,"
said Janet warmly. "Christmas dinner didn't feel
right without you."

Everyone joined in, then, clamouring to tell
Rachel their news. It felt like coming home to
your own family, Rachel thought, tears pricking
her eyelids. After all the terrible things that had
happened, and the cloud she had been under, it
was so wonderful to be needed again, to be liked
and welcomed and trusted.

Nina gave Rachel a long, appraising look. "Poor
Rachel – we haven't even given you a chance to
get a cup of coffee. Sit down. Let me butter you a

croissant." That made everyone suddenly turn concerned eyes on to Rachel. Concerned – and curious.

"By the way, where were you actually?" Jonquil demanded, speaking for all of them.

This was her moment and Rachel was not planning to waste it. She drew the little velvet pouch out of her pocket. "Oh, I just went to find something I thought you might be needing," she said casually. Then she handed the package to Jonquil.

Jonquil stared at the pouch with unbelieving eyes. Almost not daring to, she opened the little bag and shook its contents into her hand. She gasped. "My precious work! My musical sequence! My treasures!" With shining eyes she looked up at Rachel. "But how – how did you find them?"

Rachel grinned happily. "It's a long story," she told her, "and I haven't got time to tell you now. Haven't you got an appointment this morning?"

Jonquil clapped her hand dramatically to her forehead. "Of course! Tommy – we must rush at once. I'll just go and slip into something more, er, powerful. Rachel, how can I thank you? I just know, now, my meeting's going to be successful. It's an omen. The sequence has returned to me and he's going to buy it. Darling!" She emphasized the word with a little pouting kiss into the air, then dramatically swept out of the room.

It was only when she'd gone that the others filled Rachel in on the dramas of Christmas Day. Alex, it transpired, was in hospital with a broken leg. Lisa was with him. Rachel, wondering how many more dramas there could possibly be, rushed back to her apartment. Before she did anything else, she had to try to speak to Jack.

She rang his private number but there was no reply. She tried to get through to him through the hotel switchboard, but the friendly receptionist, sounding sympathetic but unhelpful, just informed her that Mr Woodford was unavailable.

Trying to quell her growing sense of unease, Rachel rushed round to Northern Heights. Perhaps Jack had left a message for her there. He hadn't. Marjorie herself was on duty at the office. She was unusually sweet to Rachel. "My dear," she greeted her. "So glad you've returned. Naturally I was rather disturbed at your sudden disappearance but I understand you've found the missing jewels, so that's wonderful news. Now, I'm sure you'll be wanting to see that poor young man with the broken leg, so why don't I drive you to the hospital? And you can tell me all about your adventures on the way."

Rachel found it a great relief to pour out her story to Marjorie – who was shocked, impressed and amazed at all the right moments, tut-tutting, gasping, and occasionally exclaiming, "No! Really? She didn't! She couldn't!"

"What a very surprising turn of events," she commented at last, which Rachel thought was rather a feeble summing-up of the whole adventure. "And what a very disturbed young woman poor Gudrun must be. Well, dear, let's look on the bright side. At least you've proved your innocence once and for all."

"It would have been nice if people had believed in me all along," muttered Rachel.

Marjorie gave her a sharp glance. "Yes, well, that may be the case, dear, but circumstances were against you, weren't they? And after all, we have our clients to consider. You know what I always say."

"We at Dream Ticket put our clients first," chanted Rachel in a bored voice. "We like to think of them as part of our family." Then she remembered how kind and welcoming her own chalet had been that morning, and completely without warning, she burst into tears.

Marjorie, who had just arrived at the hospital, pulled up in the little forecourt and turned her attention full on Rachel. She had suddenly transformed once again – this time, from stern manageress to kindly matron.

"Oh, my dear!" she exclaimed, full of concern. "How stupid of me! Of course, you've been through a great deal, so brave, rescuing the girl who has been persecuting you. Quite the heroine, really. It's bound to catch up with you!"

Still fussing, her arm round Rachel, she led her to the hospital waiting room and managed to find a steaming cup of delicious coffee. "Now you wait here and drink that," she ordered her. "Then you can go and see your friend. Meanwhile, I'll try and contact headquarters to find out more about young Gudrun. And I think a few words with Mr Woodford may be in order, too."

Lisa was sitting by Alex's bed, holding his hand and staring at his sleeping face, urging him to

163

wake up. Her heart was in turmoil. Ever since she had witnessed the horrifying sight of Alex careening headlong into the snow, Lisa had been jolted back into her senses. Of course it was Alex she loved – she'd loved him all along. Seeing him sprawled on the ground, so pale and still, had caused a renewed rush of tenderness and concern in her. Now all she wanted to do was talk to him, tell him she loved him, and make up for all the dark moments of doubt.

His eyes flickered, then opened. When he saw her his face broke into a smile. "Lisa! Is it still Christmas?"

She shook her head. "Sorry, no – we both missed the dinner. You were having an emergency operation to set your leg and I was having kittens. But I saved you this." She produced a paper hat, and fixed it on to his head. "Oh, and I wasn't sure about the hospital food, so I've brought you some muesli."

Alex curled up his nose. "I hate muesli."

"But it's good for you," fussed Lisa. "You really should look after yourself better, Alex. It drives me to a frenzy, worrying about all that rubbish you put inside you."

Alex grinned happily. "I love it when you fret about my diet," he told her. "It's not going to do much good. But I like to know you care." Lisa punched him playfully in the ribs and he winced, then doubled up.

"Ouch! I have just broken my leg, you know!"

"Sorry!" she gasped, appalled. "Did I hurt you? Are you OK? Shall I get the nurse?"

Alex lay back gingerly. "No, I think I'll be all right. As long as I keep perfectly still and don't get excited."

Lisa gave him a sly look. "Oh, dear. I'm not sure if that's going to be totally possible," she said sweetly. Then leaned over and kissed him.

"Mmm," he murmured. "That was worth hurting for! Hey, guess what?"

"What?" asked Lisa, snuggling against him.

"The doctor told me it's a really bad break. I won't be out of here for weeks. He says it's imperative that I don't move."

"Oh, dear," said Lisa happily. "Does that mean you have to stay here for a long time?"

"Ever, probably," agreed Alex.

"That's terrible," said Lisa, a smile spreading over her face.

There was a shuffling and a coughing sound. They looked up to see Rachel standing in the doorway. "Great," she said. "A captive audience. How are you, Alex?"

"Oh, you know – terrible," Alex shrugged. "But OK apart from that."

"Good. So you're well enough to hear a long, long story."

When Rachel had finished, Alex whistled. "Wow – that makes a broken leg seem quite tame," he commented. Lisa was looking thoughtful.

"You know, there's something that just doesn't make sense," she said slowly. "Remember my terrible excursion up the ski lift. The day all the runs had the wrong flags? Doesn't it sound terribly to you like Gudrun's work?"

"I suppose so," agreed Rachel. "But why would Gudrun want to get at you? It doesn't really add up, does it? Unless she just hated you for being friends with me."

"No – there had to be more to it," said Lisa. "You know, she started acting strangely to me before that. Just before that…" She paused, thinking hard.

"I know when it was!" she said finally. "I was helping Jason to look for his key-ring. Gudrun found us together in the locker room by the pool. I wonder – do you suppose she was jealous of me? Because she saw me with him?"

Rachel shook her head. "I doubt it. It's Jack she's in love with. Jason was just a front." Then, remembering Jack, she fell silent. If only she could speak to him. Was he avoiding her, because she'd disappeared last night? Had he somehow fallen back in love with Gudrun after all?

"It's definitely Jack she wants," Rachel repeated sadly. "What I'd like to know is, what's he going to do about it?"

After Marjorie had dropped her off at Northern Heights, Rachel decided to go and find Karl. She wanted to thank him for driving her to the station yesterday. And, she admitted to herself, she wanted the comfort of his flattery, his easy flirtation, his warmth, his welcome.

The bar was closed, as it was not yet midday. The pâtisserie was open, but Karl was nowhere to be seen. "Can I go through the back?" Rachel asked the young woman behind the counter. "I'm a friend of Karl's. I just wanted to call on him."

She made her way through the warm kitchen, breathing in the heavenly scent of freshly baking bread and melting chocolate. Then she was squeezing through the narrow path that led to Karl's house and garden. She stopped short when she heard voices. They were coming from the hot tub, right near the house.

"I want you to have a special treat, after all you have been through," Karl was saying, his voice heavy with sincerity. "Let me help you to relax."

"This is heaven," said a second, female voice. "So hot, and all round us it's so cold."

"Yes, but you must learn to sink into the sensation." That was Karl again. Rachel could imagine his hands, kneading the back of the woman's neck, working on the knots of stress in her shoulders, just as he had with her.

She peered round a little – just enough to catch a glimpse of the woman's face. It was Nina. Rachel smiled. How foolish of her to think that Karl would save his routine just for her.

She slipped quietly away and back to Northern Heights. Marjorie caught sight of her and called over from the office: "Most mysterious, dear! I simply can't get hold of Jack Woodford. Nobody knows where he is. It seems he's disappeared."

Feeling even more desolate, Rachel decided to go for a swim. The pool was empty, and it was good to be able to let out all her feelings as she ploughed through the water with strong, steady strokes, length after length after length.

She was completely caught up in the sensation of thrashing through the water, her eyes blurry, her heart pounding, when she heard a voice floating towards her. "Rachel! Rachel – it's me!"

Hardly able to believe her ears, she looked up at the shadowy figure standing by the pool, fully dressed. She shook her head, scattering water everywhere. Could it be – could it really be him?

"Jack?" she ventured timorously. "How did you know I was here?"

The figure bent down so that she could see his face, very near to hers. He was smiling. "Easy," he answered. "That's what you always do when you're worried or angry. Remember how many times you used to plunge into that pool in Spain?"

"But – what are you doing here?" she asked, still bewildered. And then, somehow, she was out of the water and in his arms.

"Hey, listen – it's fine if you want to get water all over my new jumper," he joked. "Really! Ever since I met you I've bought only waterproof things." Not really understanding why, Rachel found she was crying again – crying and laughing at the same time as Jack held her close and said: "I didn't actually bargain for salt water, but go right ahead."

A little while later, the two of them lay side by side in the sauna. "The best way I can think of to warm up after a gruelling six-hour train journey," Jack said, luxuriating in the intense, dry heat.

"But why didn't you tell me you were coming?" asked Rachel.

"Huh!" he retorted. "Why didn't you tell me you were leaving?"

So Rachel sighed, and told him everything that had happened since they'd said goodbye in the hospital in Grossburg. He listened intently, nodding from time to time.

"Well, I can't exactly pretend I was delighted to find you'd vanished again," he said. "I thought maybe you'd had enough of me." They squeezed hands, able to laugh now at the very idea. "But all *I* wanted was to be with you again. So I came chasing after you. I'm not surprised at what you've told me," he added gravely. "In fact, Gudrun told me most of it herself, in the end."

"Really?" asked Rachel, in surprise.

"Rachel, you have to understand that Gudrun is very seriously ill," Jack said. "She has a severe personality disorder – far worse than I'd ever thought. Oh, I knew she was very jealous and had an awful temper. But I honestly never believed she would be capable of such sabotage. She's deluded herself into believing that I'd come back to her, if only she could get rid of you. She even boasted about what she'd done to you. She thought it might make me love her more, to know what she was prepared to do to get me."

"She didn't mention Lisa, did she?" asked Rachel idly.

"Oh, yes," answered Jack. "She reckoned Lisa was after some guy called Jason. She boasted that Lisa didn't have a chance because Jason was besotted with her. She's very possessive, you know – even if she hasn't the slightest interest in the person. It was enough for her that Lisa seemed to be trying to steal something that belonged to her. So she decided to punish her."

"She told you that?" asked Rachel, incredulous.

"Well, not exactly," admitted Jack. "She's now been moved to the psychiatric wing of the hospital. And she told them. Apparently she's the most exciting psychotic they've admitted for years. Poor Gudrun..."

It was New Year's Eve and the Northern Heights party room was humming. This time, thought Rachel, everyone had something to celebrate. Jonquil, dressed in satin and feathers from head to toe, was shimmying all over the dance floor with Tommy. Both looked ecstatic. The buyer from Switzerland had fallen in love with her designs, especially the musical ones. He had placed a huge order there and then, and even promised her an exhibition in his gallery.

"And it's you I have to thank, darling," she'd said to Rachel. "It would never have happened without you."

Now, swaying towards Rachel, she blew her a happy kiss. "Wonderful party, darling," she said. "Wonderful party, wonderful holiday. Wonderful chalet. And oh, by the way, did I tell you I'm an auntie? Cerise has finally gone and had the baby and they've called it Constance. Isn't that a joke!"

The music was fifties rock and roll, and Sean and Janet were jiving wildly. As Sean threw her through his legs, up again and right into the air, she was squealing with sheer pleasure. Rachel thought this confident, attractive, fun-loving girl was almost unrecognizable as the sullen, clumsy wife of only a few days before.

Even Jason had transformed. He'd been very shocked when Rachel had broken the news to him about Gudrun. But he'd had help recovering. Tammy was there now, clinking glasses with him and pulling him on to the dance floor. She was looking very happy. "Astrologers love the new year," she explained to Rachel as they passed her. "It's when the planets are most likely to come together in happy convergence."

"Just like us?" asked a twinkling Marjorie, who was flirting wildly with a new ski instructor.

"Just like us," echoed Jack, looking at his watch. It was just coming up to midnight. The whole party shouted out the final seconds of the year. "FIVE ... FOUR ... THREE ... TWO ... ONE!" Then the lights came on, a flock of balloons were released on to the floor, everyone screamed, "Happy New Year!"

Jason took Tammy in his arms and kissed her. She was warm and responsive, loving and sensual. Somehow, the memories of Gudrun seemed to slip away, just as ice melts when the sun comes out.

Still imprisoned in his hospital bed, Alex reached out for Lisa. "Happy New Year," he said, as they kissed. "Just promise me I don't have to do anything healthy again. Look where it got me this time."

"Nothing at all, unless you count this," answered Lisa, pouring each of them a glass of champagne.

"Happy New Year," Karl said to Nina. "To the most beautiful woman I have ever seen." They kissed, and she grinned.

"Happy New Year, you old fraud," she said lightly.

Jack held Rachel close, and kissed her, then handed her a tiny box. Inside was a ring. "Make it a really happy new year?" he asked gently. And once more they were kissing, she was crying, the room was swaying – and Rachel, clasped in his strong embrace, was filled with all the joy and longing and dreams and hope that a new year is meant to bring.